R. L. STINE

CAN YOU KEEP A SECRET?

A *FEAR STREET* NOVEL

THOMAS DUNNE BOOKS
ST. MARTIN'S GRIFFIN
NEW YORK

THOMAS DUNNE BOOKS.
An imprint of St. Martin's Press.

CAN YOU KEEP A SECRET? Copyright © 2016 by Parachute Publishing, LLC. All rights reserved. Printed in the United States of America. For information, address St. Martin's Press, 175 Fifth Avenue, New York, N.Y. 10010.

www.thomasdunnebooks.com
www.stmartins.com

The Library of Congress Cataloging-in-Publication Data is available upon request.

ISBN 978-1-250-05894-2 (hardcover)
ISBN 978-1-250-10102-0 (international, sold outside the U.S., subject to rights availability)
ISBN 978-1-4668-9295-8 (e-book)

Our books may be purchased in bulk for promotional, educational, or business use. Please contact your local bookseller or the Macmillan Corporate and Premium Sales Department at 1-800-221-7945, extension 5442, or by e-mail at MacmillanSpecialMarkets@macmillan.com.

First U.S. Edition: April 2016
First International Edition: April 2016

10 9 8 7 6 5 4 3 2 1

For Joan and Jean . . . sisters . . .
but not as scary as the ones in this book

1.

In my dream, I'm running through mud, my pale night-gown flapping. I can hear the *splat splat splat* of my bare feet as they slap the soft, wet ground.

I run through puddles of cold water, and I can feel the cold even though I'm completely aware that I'm dreaming. I know that the whispers I hear are the leaves on the trees shivering in a stiff, warm wind.

I feel the wind on my face, and I hear the whispers all around behind the *splat splat* of my bare feet, kicking up the mud, sending it splashing like waves on both sides of me.

I see the crescent moon in the purple sky above the shimmering trees. It looks like a sideways smile, and it reminds me of the silver moon pendant on the chain around my neck.

The moon seems so close in my dream, as if I could reach up and squeeze my hand around it. But I can't slow down to grab the moon. I'm being chased. And I know if I turn around, I'll see *it*.

And even though I know that, I can't keep from turning back. In my dreams, I'm never in control. I can't do what I'd like to do.

I'm running barefoot in the wet mud under the low, leafy tree branches. I'm scared. I know that I'm scared. And that I have good reason.

Because when I turn around . . . when I take a quick, shuddering glance behind me . . . the wolf is there. The black wolf of my dreams.

It grunts and snarls as it trots silently behind me. It lowers its head as if preparing to attack. The black fur on its back bristles. And once again, I see its eyes. Blue like mine. The black wolf has my eyes.

I have black hair and blue eyes, and I'm dreaming about a wolf with black fur and blue eyes. And I tell myself in my dream that I'm not crazy. People have nightmares. People have the same dream over and over.

But most people don't dream of animals with *their* eyes. And why does it make me so frightened? I'm asleep but I can feel the butterfly flitting of my heartbeats.

I gaze at the wolf. Our blue eyes meet and lock on one another. Its long snout quivers. Thick white drool oozes from the sides of its mouth. The black wolf bares its teeth and utters a low menacing growl from deep in its throat that sounds like choking, like someone spewing.

I want to look away. But the eyes hold me, paralyze me.

And suddenly, *I* am the wolf.

I am the wolf. I am the black wolf.

In my dream, I become the wolf, staring, my eyes locked on the other wolf.

We attack. We wrestle. We snarl and rage and spit and drool. We bite and claw and bump heads and tear at each other.

I am fierce. I am exploding with anger. Exploding.

I wake up screaming. I try to leap out of bed. Tangled in the bedsheet, I tumble to the floor. Land with a soft *thud* on my side.

I'm panting. My heart skipping up and down in my chest. I blink several times, blinking the dream away. Forcing away the lingering pictures, the face of the wolf . . . the anger . . . the blue eyes.

I'm in my room. Silvery moonlight floods in through the open window.

"Hey," I mutter, still shaking away the frightening images. "Hey. Another nightmare. A nightmare. That's all."

A voice from across the bedroom startles me. "What's wrong?"

My sister Sophie sits up. Sophie and I share the room. Sophie's eyes catch the moonlight from the window. She has blue eyes, too.

"Another nightmare," I tell her, still shaky.

"You had your wolf dream again?" She crosses the room to me and places a warm hand on my shoulder.

I nod. "Yes. Again."

She gazes over my shoulder and her eyes go wide. Her mouth drops open. She steps past me and leans over my bed.

"Emmy? Why are your sheets all torn and shredded?"

2.

felt a shudder run down my body. I turned and stared at the ripped-up sheets. Sophie clicked on the bedside table lamp, and we both stared in silence.

My brain whirred. I struggled to explain it. I felt as if I were still in the dream. I kept trying to wake up, to pull myself out of it.

Sophie hugged me. Her short black hair was damp, matted to her forehead. She's fifteen, two years younger than me. But we look like twins. The same high cheekbones, pale skin, and blue eyes. That's why she cut her hair so short and severe, shaved on one side. Because mine flows down past my shoulders. She just got so tired of people calling her by my name, Emmy.

"These awful dreams . . ." she started, letting me go and taking a step back, her face filled with concern.

But my eyes were on the window. "Sophie? Wasn't that window closed when we went to sleep?"

She turned. "I don't know. I guess so. I don't really remember."

I gazed at the window, at the silvery crescent moon high in the sky. A gust of cold wind ruffled my hair. And I shivered again.

It took a long time to get back to sleep. And Mom woke me up too early the next morning, clanking around in the kitchen. Why couldn't she wait to unload the dishwasher? Did it really have to be done at seven on a Saturday morning?

I pulled on the faded jeans I'd worn the day before and a T-shirt that didn't look too wrinkled and hurried to the kitchen. Mom leaned over the white Formica counter in her bathrobe, hair unbrushed, having her breakfast cigarette. She has one cigarette first thing in the morning and one after dinner. Two a day. She tells everyone she doesn't smoke.

Dad says she should drink an extra cup of coffee in the morning, and she wouldn't need the cigarette. He's the practical one in the family. I guess that's why no one ever listens to him.

Actually, Sophie is a lot like Dad. They're both soft-spoken and quiet and would rather sit in a corner and read a book than go out, and Sophie is just like that. Mom and I are the social ones. I always wonder if most families are divided into two camps.

"Mom, I had the wolf dream again," I said. I cleared my throat. My voice was still clogged with sleep.

Mom stubbed out the cigarette. She blew a strand of hair off her forehead. Mom has straw-blonde hair and brown eyes. She doesn't look at all like Sophie and me.

She shook her head. "Ever since you were five . . ." she started. She sighed. "Ever since you were five and that dog bit you. . . . that's when the dreams started."

"I know," I said. "Tell me something I don't know."

Mom stood up straight. "You don't have to be sharp with me. I only meant—"

"We keep having the same conversation," I said, trying not be so shrill. "How come I don't remember being bitten by a dog?"

Mom fiddled with the belt on her black-and-white-checked robe. "You were so young, Emmy. How much do you remember from when you were five?"

"I remember some things," I said. "I remember some things that happened in Kindergarten. But a dog bite . . . Mom, you'd think I'd remember something as frightening as that."

"You've blocked it from your memory, dear," she said, finally raising her eyes to mine. "We've talked about this. Such a painful thing. People block memories like that. They don't want to think about them."

"But, Mom—"

"Don't you remember anything?" she asked. "We were overseas. Visiting your Great Aunt Marta in that little farm village outside Prague? I wasn't there at the time. But Marta

9

saw it happen. That dog came leaping out from the trees and attacked you. And she—"

Sophie stumbled noisily into the room, coughing and clearing her throat, her bare feet clomping on the yellow tiles. She twitched her nose and sniffled a few times. "I think I have a cold."

"It's your allergies," I said. "You get your spring allergies every year, and you always forget."

She coughed again. "How come *you* don't have spring allergies?"

"It's not like we're twins," I said. "I don't have to have everything you have. Duh."

Mom poured a cup of coffee from the coffeemaker. "Sophie, you were there with Aunt Marta that day," she said. "Do you remember when the dog came out of the forest and bit Emmy?"

Sophie rolled her eyes. "Are we having this talk again? Mom, I was only three. How am I supposed to remember anything?"

I didn't want to continue this discussion, but I felt so frustrated. I had a strong feeling that Mom wasn't telling the whole truth. I knew she wouldn't lie to me. But her explanation of why I've had these frightening wolf dreams just didn't totally add up.

"Where's the scar?" I demanded. I lifted my right leg and pulled up the jeans by the cuff. "You said it bit my leg. But where's the scar?"

"It healed," Mom said. She twirled the coffee mug in her hand. "You were lucky. It healed pretty quickly."

I stared at her. The radio behind us at the table droned in the background. Two voices discussing the news, I think. "But, Mom," I insisted. *Why couldn't I just let it go?* "I keep dreaming about wolves—not dogs."

She brushed her hair back with one hand. "Dr. Goldman can explain it better than me," she said. "I don't know why you keep refusing to see him. Sometimes in our dreams we make our fears even more horrifying than in real life. In your dreams, you turn the dog into a wolf. But that doesn't mean—"

"Ssshh." I raised my hand to silence Mom. The voice on the radio had caught my attention. I moved closer so I could hear better.

"What's wrong?" Mom asked.

"Sssshhh." I leaned toward the little black table radio.

"The attack occurred last night in Shadyside Park behind the high school," a man was saying. "Delmar Hawkins of North Hills reported the attack to police. Hawkins said that he was walking his dog along the path toward the river when a large black wolf jumped out from the trees and attacked the dog. Police confirmed that the dog was killed in a most ferocious manner. Police have begun a search of the park for the black wolf, and a helicopter unit has been sent for. Meanwhile . . ."

The voice continued, but the reporter's words were meaningless to me. Just a blur of sound. I suddenly felt cold all over, as if my blood had frozen inside me.

My thoughts were crazy. I dreamed about that black wolf last night. And at the same time that I was dreaming, a *real* black wolf appeared in Shadyside Park. A real black wolf came out of the trees and killed a man's dog.

Of course, that had nothing to do with me. Of course, it had to be a totally weird coincidence.

So why was I trembling so hard? Why did I feel so strange?

"Emmy? What's wrong?" Sophie's voice broke into my thoughts.

I didn't answer. I suddenly remembered my bedsheets. All shredded. I grabbed Mom's hands and tugged her away from the kitchen counter. Her hands were warm. Mine were ice cold.

"Mom—come with me," I said. "I have to show you something."

She tugged her hands free. "Don't pull me. I'm coming. What's your problem, Emmy?"

"I'll show you," I said, leading the way down the back hall. "You have to see this, Mom."

"Okay, okay. I'm coming."

"My dream last night . . . I was running in the woods," I said, suddenly breathless. "Barefoot. Running in mud. And when I woke up . . . the sheets . . . they were torn . . . all shredded and wrecked."

Mom didn't say anything. I heard Sophie sneezing back in the kitchen. I grabbed Mom's arm and pulled her to my bed. "Look."

We both stared at the tangle of sheets on my bed. My mouth dropped open. My breath caught in my throat.

The sheets were perfectly okay.

3.

Sophie appeared in the bedroom doorway, a Kleenex wadded in one hand. "This is getting too weird," she said. She crossed to my bed, grabbed the sheets, and tugged them, making them billow like sails. "You should listen to Mom, Emmy, and go see Dr. Goldman."

I started to protest. But the words wouldn't come.

Am I seriously crazy?

"B-but . . . Sophie," I stammered, finally finding my voice. "You saw the sheets ripped up. When I woke you up. You saw it, too."

"Huh? You didn't wake me up." She studied me, her expression sympathetic . . . caring. I could see she was worried about me. "It must have been part of your dream, Em. I didn't see your sheets or anything."

Again, I had that cold feeling. I followed them to the kitchen. Mom offered to make scrambled eggs, but I didn't feel hungry. I sat down at the table and filled a bowl with corn flakes. But I didn't reach for the milk.

"Let's change the subject," Mom said, forcing her "cheerful" voice. "What are you doing today?"

"I'm going to the library to work on my Asian Studies report," Sophie said. Sophie's second home is the library. She has a special place behind the stacks in the main reading room where she likes to sit on the floor and spread out all her papers and read and write. The librarians know her. She's like their pet. I can't understand why she likes to be alone so much of the time. But she does.

I guess that's the biggest difference between us. I can't *stand* to be alone. I'm a social person. I like friends and boyfriends and hanging out with crowds of people and partying and laughing and having fun.

Sophie is prettier than me. I really think so. But she's never had a serious boyfriend. I can't talk to her about it. She just clams up when I mention it.

"And what are you doing today?" Mom had turned to me.

The radio voices droned on. Some kind of call-in show. Were they talking about the wolf attack? I didn't want to hear anymore. I clicked it off.

Who listens to radio these days anyway? No one. Only my dad. He always has to have a radio on. And he collects old radios, like from the nineteen forties and fifties. Weird-looking but he loves them. He loves fiddling with them, fixing them, polishing them up, and getting them to work.

Mom was waiting for me to answer her question. "I have

to bring Eddie his backpack," I told her. "He left it at the gym yesterday."

Mom frowned. She always frowns when I mention Eddie.

"Eddie started his new job this morning," I said. "At the pet cemetery in Martinsville."

"What a horrible job," Mom said, making a face.

"I know. It's yucky," I said. "But he really needs the money. Especially since his stepdad was suspended from the police force."

"He deserved to be suspended," Mom said, twirling her coffee mug again. "He beat up that teenager for no reason."

I groaned. "Mom, you know that's not true. He thought the kid had a gun. He made a mistake, but—"

"I don't know why you got mixed up with Eddie and that Kovacs family," Mom interrupted. "Danny Franklin is such a nice guy."

"Mom, give Emmy a break," Sophie chimed in. "You *know* that Danny broke up with Emmy. Emmy didn't break up with him. Now he's going out with Callie Newman."

Mom squinted at me. "So you had to immediately start going out with his best friend?"

I wasn't enjoying this conversation. I could feel the anger growing in my chest. I tried to hold back, but I couldn't. I exploded. "None of your business, Mom," I screamed. "Eddie can't help it if he isn't rich. You're a total snob."

Of course, standing there, tugging at the sides of my hair, feeling my anger burn my chest, I had no way of knowing that in a few short hours, Eddie and I would be *incredibly* rich.

4.

I tossed Eddie's backpack into the backseat and climbed into Mom's Corolla. Mom teaches English at the private Boys' Academy in Dover Falls, a few towns south of Shadyside. Her school let out in May, and Mom is taking the summer off and mostly staying at home. Which means the car is basically mine.

It was a hot, hazy day. It felt more like summer than spring, and the sky was an eerie yellow above the mist that clung to the road. Still early on a Saturday morning. There wasn't much traffic after I got out of Shadyside.

Martinsville is a small industrial town about fifteen minutes away. I always picture blue-and-white uniforms whenever I think of the town. The Martinsville Blue Devils are our big rival in football and basketball.

Eddie told me the pet cemetery was on the outskirts just past the old dairy, where the highway narrows. I found it easily. I followed a narrow dirt road along a brick wall up to the tall iron gates where a stenciled sign read: PET HEAVEN.

I saw only one car parked in the small lot, a beat-up old Pontiac with the rear window cracked. I parked a few spaces away from it, hoisted up Eddie's backpack, and headed to the main gate.

I saw Eddie through the tall metal fence that stretched on both sides of the gate. He was bent over the handle of a shovel, mopping his forehead with the sleeve of his shirt. He turned to the fence when he heard me calling to him.

He brushed back his wavy brown hair. His face was red, from work, I guessed. He didn't smile. Eddie almost never smiles. But he gave me a wave and motioned me to the gate.

Eddie has slate gray eyes that don't look real. People think he wears contacts, but he doesn't. People notice his eyes right away.

He's lanky and tall and his serious expression makes him look more like a man than a boy. He has a scar on his chin that he doesn't remember how he got, and it makes him look a little tough. But he's generally calm and has a soft voice and an easy manner. He's very confident. Little things don't bother him.

I think that's why we're a good couple. Sometimes I can be like an emotional volcano, and he's always smooth and steady. When I'm feeling really troubled about something, he always knows how to calm me down.

Ha. Here I am talking like we're an old married couple.

I should be talking about how I don't really know Eddie. I mean, we've been going together for less than a month.

Eddie was watching me, waiting for me to enter the pet cemetery. I grabbed the handle to the gate—and stopped.

I felt a sudden chill. A coldness in the air . . . I couldn't tell where it was coming from. My senses felt alert. A kind of warning. My skin bristled, as if all my nerves were standing on end.

I let go of the gate handle and gazed around. No one there. I couldn't see anything that would make me feel this frightened.

But I felt it. I felt I was in the grip of something very wrong.

I suddenly realized I was holding my breath. Holding it against a strong, putrid odor that seemed to be pouring through the entrance gate.

What smells so awful here?

"Emmy? What's up?" Eddie's shout burst into my thoughts.

I took a deep breath, pulled open the gate, and stepped inside. The backpack stuck on the iron frame and I had to tug it free. The gate slammed behind me as I hurried over to Eddie.

"Eddie, there's something wrong here," I said breathlessly. "I don't think you should work in this place."

His strange gray eyes flashed. "Hello to you, too," he said softly.

"I'm sorry. Hello," I said. "But there's something evil here, Eddie. I can feel it."

He shrugged his slender shoulders. "It's a cemetery, Emmy. There's a lot of dead dogs and cats here. It's not supposed to be the Magic Kingdom."

"I-I know," I stammered. I was beginning to doubt my own strong feeling. But the cold lingered on the back of my neck, and the sickening smell had grown even stronger on this side of the fence.

"Thanks for bringing the backpack," Eddie said. "You can drop it by that tree." He pointed. He turned and strode back to a rectangle of dirt between two low gravestones. "Mac has me digging a grave. It's like a hundred degrees. I'm totally drenched in sweat."

"Is that what smells so bad?" I said, making a joke.

"Funny," he muttered. He dug the shovel blade into the dirt.

"Mac is your boss?" I asked.

He nodded. "Yeah. And he owns the place. That's his office over there." He motioned with his head to a two-story shingle building across the field. "Mac lives above the office. Do you believe it? He lives in a pet cemetery."

"Weird," I said. Then I saw the large green trash bag under a tree. "Eddie," I said, "what's in that? Is it—?"

"Yeah. A dead dog," he said. "Killed last night."

I blinked. "Oh, wow. Last night?"

Eddie tossed a shovelful of dirt aside. "The owner said it was attacked by a wolf." He turned to me. "Do you believe that? A wolf in Shadyside Park? So close to your house?"

He kept his gaze on me. "Hey, Emmy? What's wrong? You're shaking like a leaf."

5.

Before I could answer, I heard a shout. Eddie and I both turned to the voice. I saw a big man in a baggy gray sweats trotting toward us. "Hey, how's it going?" he called.

Eddie introduced him. Mac Stanton, the owner of the place. He was tall and wide with a big pouch of a belly poking against his sweatshirt. He had a perfectly round face with a shaved head, a silver ring in his right ear, and a black neck tattoo I couldn't make out.

"Hey, Emmy—welcome to Pet Heaven." He had a hoarse voice, scratchy and kind of high. His smile revealed a gold tooth in front. "I'm putting this dude to work." He slapped Eddie on the shoulder.

"I'm almost finished with this one, Mac," Eddie said, mopping the sweat off his forehead again.

Mac studied the hole Eddie had dug, rubbing his double chins with stubby fingers. "I think a foot deeper," he said. He pressed a fist into his back and stretched. "Normally,

I'd help you out with this. But I got a kink in my back."
He winked at me. "I don't want to tell you how I got it."

"No problem," Eddie said, shifting the shovel to his
other hand. "I'm just happy to have the job, Mac. You
know my family needs the money right now."

Mac nodded. He rubbed his shaved head. "I gotta get
out of the sun. I stroke easily." He laughed at his own joke.
"Nice meetin' you, Emmy," he said. He turned and started
to trot back toward the office.

"He's kind of rough, but he's a nice guy," Eddie said.

I watched Eddie dig the grave a foot deeper. It didn't take
long. I stared at the bulging trash bag. I pictured a big wolf
attacking the dog. The wolf was black. Just my imagination
again. Dreams don't come true. Sensible Me knew that.
But . . .

Eddie climbed out of the grave with a groan. Wiping his
sweaty hands on the legs of his jeans, he grabbed the trash
bag. He started to slide it down into the grave.

"Whoa!" He cried out as the bag broke. The dead dog
tumbled onto the ground at my feet.

I let out a cry and stumbled back. The dog corpse was
stiff and it already smelled sour. A black Lab, so messed up
I could barely recognize it as a dog. Its eyes had sunken
deep into their sockets. The fur . . . the fur . . . the fur on
its back had been clawed away. Patches of dried blood clung
to the shreds. The skin underneath was red and raw.

Like a hunk of rotting meat.

"Ohhhhh." A moan escaped my throat. I couldn't help it. I couldn't take my eyes off the disgusting thing.

But I couldn't stand it. My stomach lurched hard and I started to gag.

"Are you okay?" I heard Eddie call to me. But he suddenly seemed far away. "Are you okay?"

No, I *wasn't* okay.

"Urrrrrrp." I forced my lunch down, swallowing hard. And holding my hands over my mouth, I spun around and ran.

6.

I wrapped my arm around a slender tree trunk. Panting, swallowing frantically, I forced myself not to vomit. The putrid smell lingered in my nose, and I couldn't blink away the sight of that pink, furless body, covered in scratches and streaks of dried blood.

My whole body trembled. The waves of nausea wouldn't quit. I pressed myself against the tree trunk, holding on tightly as if hanging on for dear life.

The dog was skinned. Skinned alive.

And much as I tried to force it from my mind, my dream of last night played itself once again in my mind. And I saw the black wolf with its terrifying blue eyes, saw it paw the muddy ground, snarling and drooling, baring its teeth. Saw it leap to the attack with a shrill cry from deep in its animal throat. Clawing and biting furiously.

Just a dream.

But I was a wolf in the dream. I was the blue-eyed wolf with the raven-black hair. I was the one on the attack.

This poor dog had died at the same time I was a wolf in my dream.

Am I making a crazy connection?

"Of course I am," I told myself. "What possible connection could there be?"

A coincidence. A frightening coincidence.

Stop scaring yourself with crazy thoughts, Emmy.

I started to feel a little better. My stomach was still churning. But the waves of nausea had faded. My heartbeat returned to normal.

I turned to find Eddie behind me, his face solemn and filled with concern. "Emmy? You okay? I'm sorry you had to see that dog corpse. It upset you?"

I nodded. "Yeah. It was so . . . red and raw."

"Well, it's gone," he said, placing a hand on my shoulder. "I buried it." He blinked. He had drops of sweat in his eyelashes. The sun was lowering itself behind the trees. But the air still felt hot and humid.

"I'm outta here," Eddie said. "Come with me. I have to ask Mac something."

He carried the shovel in one hand and kept the other arm around my shoulders as we walked through the rows of low gravestones to the office at the top of the sloping hill. Mac stood outside the glass door, leaning against the wall, his thumbs tapping rapidly on his phone.

He kept tapping for a long while, then finally looked up. "Eddie, dude—you finished?"

Eddie nodded. "Yeah. Where does the shovel go, Mac?"

Mac pointed. "Just rest it against the side of the building. I'll see you Monday after school, right?"

"Yeah," Eddie said. He hesitated. "Listen, Mac . . . I have to ask you a favor."

Mac lowered his phone to the pocket of his gray sweatpants. He squinted at Eddie. "Favor?"

Eddie glanced at me. He was normally so confident, but I could see he was nervous. "Mac, do you think I could have an advance on my pay?"

Mac's expression didn't change. He kept squinting at Eddie with his narrow dark eyes. Finally, he said, "You're joking, right?"

"No—" Eddie started.

"You just started today," Mac said. "You dug one grave. And you want me to advance you your pay?"

Eddie's cheeks turned red. "I'm seriously desperate, Mac. I'm totally broke. I—"

"Here," Mac said. He pulled a ragged leather wallet from the sweatpants pocket. "Here. You know I'm a good guy, Eddie. Your stepdad Lou is my cousin, and I'll do what I can. Know what I mean? I mean, I gave you this job, right? Because you're blood. You're family."

Mac grinned at me. "You got a good girlfriend here, Eddie. She's class, I can tell. Not like those losers Lou told me you'd been going out with."

That made Eddie blush even deeper. He lowered his eyes but he didn't say anything.

"Here. Take this." Mac handed Eddie a ten-dollar bill.

I saw the disappointment on Eddie's face. "Mac, ten dollars won't really help," Eddie said. "Do you think—"

"Maybe Lou can fork over some money," Mac said, tucking the wallet back in his pocket.

"You *know* Lou is on suspension," Eddie said. "The police aren't paying him until after his hearing. Lou is furious about it. He doesn't have any money, Mac. He doesn't—"

"I'm real sorry. That's all I got right now, dude. Pay you next week, okay? You two have a good one." He turned and disappeared into the office.

Eddie stood with the ten-dollar bill folded in his hand. He sighed. "Oh, well. It was worth a try."

We started to walk toward my car in the front. "I guess he was trying to be nice," I said. "But his wallet was filled with cash."

Eddie frowned. "I need this job. I'm not going to start complaining about Mac."

We walked along the edge of the cemetery. The tall old trees that dotted the graveyard shimmered in the late afternoon sunlight.

Suddenly, Eddie stopped walking and turned to me. He took me by the shoulders and pulled me close. He kissed me, a long lingering kiss.

"Hey, we'll have fun tonight," he said when the kiss had ended. "You didn't tell your parents what we're going to do—did you?"

"Of course not," I said.

PART
TWO

7.

After dinner, I packed my overnight bag quickly. I knew we were going into the Fear Street Woods. But I couldn't decide what I'd need. So I just tossed in my hairbrush, a toothbrush, a sweater, and an extra pair of jeans.

The sun was almost down, and the sky outside the bedroom window was a beautiful clear violet color. A warm breeze fluttered the curtains. I felt fluttery, too. I'd never done anything like this.

Humming to myself, I stuffed a gray hoodie into the bag in case it got colder in the middle of the night. Then I struggled to zip the bulging bag. I didn't even see Sophie in the doorway. How long had she been watching me?

"Oh, hi," I said. "What's up?"

She strode into the room with her arms crossed in front of her. Her blue eyes studied me, like they were trying to pierce my brain. "Where are you *really* going?" she demanded.

I played innocent. "Huh? What do you mean?"

She lowered her hands to her waist. "You told Mom and Dad you were staying over at Rachel Martin's," she said. "But I know Rachel is away with her parents."

She had this triumphant gloating smile on her face. As if she'd just won some kind of contest. "You have to learn to stay out of my business," I said softly.

She flinched. You'd think I slapped her. Sophie always tries to confront me with things. I guess being the younger sister she feels she has to stand up for herself, or maybe prove that she's as good as I am.

She picks a fight and then she always backs down instantly. It's such a weird pattern, and it happens all the time. She never wants me to be mad at her.

Her eyes went dull and she stuck out her lips in the pouty expression she always puts on. "Emmy, you never invite me to come along on anything fun," she whined.

I frowned at her. Not this tired old speech again.

"It's because I don't have a boyfriend—isn't it," she said.

I sighed. "It's because you have to have your own friends, Sophie. You know. Your own life. I like to spend time with you—"

"No, you don't."

"Come on. I have a right to be with my friends and my boyfriend."

Her mouth dropped open and her chin trembled. I could see how angry she was. But I didn't care. I hoisted the bag onto my shoulder and edged past her and out the doorway.

CAN YOU KEEP A SECRET?

I scooted around to the passenger side so Eddie could drive my mom's car. He was in a good mood, laughing about his first day at the pet cemetery, joking about what a horrible job he had. It made me happy to see him like that. He's usually too serious about himself and obsessed with his family's problems. It was so nice to hear him laugh.

He looked ready for our all-night party in the woods. He wore a maroon-and-white Shadyside High sweatshirt over his jeans, and a baseball cap pulled down over his dark hair with the words GO, REDBIRDS across the front.

The last time he wore that cap, I asked him who the Redbirds are. He said he didn't know. He found the cap on a curb when he was walking to school.

He squealed the car onto the turn to Park Drive and gunned it. There were no other cars in sight. But I began to think maybe Eddie was *too* psyched for our adventure tonight.

I grabbed his wrist. "Slow down."

"Can't wait to get to the woods," he said. He leaned to the side and nuzzled my cheek with his lips.

"Eddie—please!" I cried, pulling away from him. "You're not watching the road." I had to shout over the music. Eddie has a Metallica Thrash Metal station on Pandora that he blasts so loud your ears wiggle. Seriously.

The sprawling houses of North Hills whirred past, their window lights yellow-orange against the darkening sky. Eddie clicked off the music. "Let's play our game," he said.

"You *are* in a good mood," I said. He only likes to play

the game when he's feeling good. I gasped. "You just went through a stop sign."

"No one around," he said. He slowed the car to make the turn onto Fear Street. "Ready to play?"

Eddie's game is called "Can You Keep a Secret?" It's not really a game at all. The rules are simple. Each of us reveals some deep, dark secret that the other one must keep forever.

I think it's fun. But it's the kind of thing Eddie usually hates. We were at a party a few months ago before we were going together, and he refused to play "Truth or Dare." Instead, he walked out of the house, shaking his head.

I was going out with his friend Danny Franklin then. Danny told me, "Eddie hates to tell people anything about himself. He likes to keep it all to himself."

"I think he's just shy," I said.

Danny shrugged and didn't reply.

The old houses on Fear Street, set way back on tree-studded lawns, were mostly dark. Eddie slowed the car as we followed the winding road to the woods.

"I'll go first," he said. "Here's my secret."

"You've enrolled in astronaut school and you plan to spend the rest of your life alone on Mars," I said.

He slapped my hand gently. "Don't try to guess. That's not the game. You're not supposed to guess." His dark eyes flashed in the light of an oncoming car. "But, yes, you're right," he said. "That's my secret."

I gave him a shove. "Seriously. What's your secret?"

His smile faded. "I don't have a driver's license. I lost my license after I was in that accident on River Ridge last month."

I stared at him, unable to hide my surprise. "For real?"

He nodded. "That's my secret. Now you have to keep it."

The trees of the Fear Street Woods rolled past, darker than the sky. Through my window, I glimpsed a sliver of a moon, still low over the trees. It looked just like the silver moon pendant I always wear, the pendant given to me by my Great Aunt Marta when I was little.

"What's your secret?" Eddie demanded. "Stop stalling."

"I wasn't stalling," I said. "I was looking at the moon."

"Emmy, you can look at the moon all night. What's your secret?"

"Well . . ." I hesitated. "You know how I've been trying not to eat meat. So . . . I have this huge craving for a cheeseburger."

Eddie laughed. "Good secret."

But I suddenly wished I hadn't said it. *I dreamed about being a wolf,* I thought. *And suddenly I have a strong craving for meat.*

That isn't like me. That isn't like me at all.

Eddie pulled the car into a cul de sac at the edge of the Fear Street Woods. He cut the engine and turned off the headlights. The thick tangle of trees in front of us disappeared in a thick, inky blackness.

The crescent moon had faded behind low clouds. I had

my window rolled down. There had been a soft, warm breeze, but it seemed to stop here. The air grew still and heavy.

I shivered. I'm not afraid of the dark, but this darkness felt eerie, as if it went on forever and would never lift. I leaned toward Eddie and he slid his arm around my shoulders.

He turned and pulled me close. I raised my face to him and he kissed me. A soft kiss, tender at first, but then more urgent, more needy. A long kiss that made me breathless.

I pulled my head back and pressed my cheek against his. We sat like that for a while, not speaking, not moving. Then Eddie raised my face with both of his hands, such warm hands, and we kissed again.

I shrieked and jerked my head back as blinding white light filled the car. And then a voice boomed into the open window: "Step out of the car slowly—and keep your hands where I can see them."

8.

Blinking in the bright light, I squeezed Eddie's hand, so hard he cried out. The light disappeared. I stared out the window, stared at Danny Franklin, a pleased grin on his face.

He stuck his head into the car. "Scared you," he said, still grinning.

I heard laughter behind him. My eyes were returning to normal. I saw Callie Newman, his new girlfriend, behind him, enjoying Danny's joke.

Danny tugged open my car door. "You should have seen the look on your face," he said.

Eddie shoved his door open, leaped out of the car, his fists curled. "I'll pound you!" he threatened, only half-serious.

Danny backed away, both hands raised. "You know I'm nonviolent. Peace. Peace!"

Yeah, right. Danny is a joker, but he's also hot-headed and impulsive, and gets in fights all the time. He's a strange combination of a fun guy who can turn angry in a second. A guy who loves to play jokes on other people but who always has to win.

Eddie says it's because Danny has red hair. "It means his head is on fire," Eddie explained once. We both laughed. We knew that wasn't very scientific.

"You two were totally getting it on," Danny teased. "Better save something for later."

"Danny, give them a break," Callie said. She grabbed Danny from behind and tugged him away. "You're about as funny as stomach cramps."

Danny laughed. "Did you just make that up?"

She rolled her eyes. "You're not the only funny one here."

"Funny looking," Eddie muttered.

Danny *is* kind of funny looking. He has his red hair shaved real short, and he has big Dumbo ears that stick straight out, light freckles on his cheeks, and a little pointed nose, with his brown eyes real close together. He'd look exactly like an elf, except he's the tallest one in our crowd.

I don't know Callie very well. She transferred to Shadyside last year. She seems really nice, and she can be funny, and she's very good with Danny. I don't blame her for stealing him away from me. Danny and I weren't getting along, and I think we were both relieved when we broke up.

Callie is very pretty, with straight straw-blonde hair, bangs across her forehead, pale green eyes, high cheekbones like a model, and a really warm, friendly smile.

She was wearing a T-shirt under a satiny black jacket and straight-legged black denim jeans that showed off how thin she is.

Eddie and Danny were having a pretend fistfight on the grass in front of the car. I gazed over Callie's shoulder and saw our two other friends at the back of Danny's SUV.

Riley Jeffers and Roxie Robinson were leaning into the hatchback trunk, pulling out camping equipment. "Hey—somebody give us a hand," Riley boomed. He's big, I mean huge, built like a middle linebacker, which he is, on the Shadyside High Tigers.

Eddie says that Riley does his strength training by crushing beer cans in his bare hands. It's true that Riley likes beer and partying, which could get him tossed off the football team. But he's also good at not getting caught.

You have to be eighteen to drink beer in Shadyside, but it's not like I know anyone who obeys the law. And now I watched Riley unload a case of Bud from the back of the SUV.

I followed Callie across the grass to greet Riley and Roxie. It's a riot to see them together, mainly because Roxie is half Riley's size. I mean, I've seen him actually pick her up and carry her around.

She likes it. She calls him "Teddy Bear," which makes the rest of us gag. But Riley smiles every time she says it.

Roxie is okay, but I think sometimes she's a little *too* cute. She has a funny lisp. She can't pronounce her *s*'s. and it makes her sound even more cute, sort of like a character in a Bugs Bunny cartoon. She looks a little rabbitlike, actually, with two front teeth that stick out and big, round brown eyes.

Roxie is into Hello Kitty, and she wears all these plastic Hello Kitty pins and plastic necklaces, and bracelets that are always clicking and jangling. Very cute. Too cute. I mean, that stuff makes my skin itch.

But she can be very sweet. When my wolf dreams got really intense last fall, I tried to confide in Sophie about them. But she just said, "Why get messed up over a couple of dreams?"

At a party at Danny's house, I pulled Roxie aside and told her about my frightening dreams, and she was totally understanding and sympathetic, and made me feel glad that I'd confided in her. Underneath all that plastic and cuteness, she's a real person.

I leaned into the back of the SUV and pulled out the bag containing a canvas tent. It was heavier than I thought, and I dropped it onto the ground, nearly smashing my feet.

"Let me get that." Riley hoisted it up easily and tossed it onto the other two tents. "Do you believe we're doing this?" he asked me.

I shook my head. "I've always wanted to camp out one night in these woods," I told him.

Roxie tugged out a lantern and set it on the ground. "Do your parents know you're here?"

I shook my head. "No way. They think I'm staying at Rachel Martin's house."

"I told my parents the football team was having a spring overnight," Riley said. "And they believed it. They believe everything I tell them."

"You have an honest face," Danny told him. "Dumb but honest."

We all laughed. Riley can always take a joke. The big Teddy Bear.

Callie shook her head. "This was Danny's idea. No way I wanted to come tonight. Camp all night in the Fear Street Woods? Hey, I may be new here, but I've heard all the stories about these woods. It's like a horror movie."

Danny uttered a ghoulish, horror-movie laugh. "We're all going to be slaughtered by a dude in a hockey mask!"

Callie shoved him hard. "How funny is that? Not." Her expression turned serious. "We must be nuts or something. Staying outdoors in the woods with a vicious wolf running wild?"

Roxie gasped. "A wolf? Seriously? What do you mean?"

"You didn't hear the news?" I said. "A wolf attacked a dog in Shadyside Park last night. The owner was walking the dog, and a wolf leaped out of the trees and chewed the dog to pieces."

Roxie's eyes grew wide. "Maybe we could move our camping stuff to my backyard. . . ."

"*Owoooooooo!*"

A loud wolf howl from right behind me made me jump. I spun around. It took me a few seconds to realize the howl came from Danny. I felt like a jerk for believing it was a real wolf. But I was a little freaked about wolves. It was easy to fool me.

Danny howled again, his cry echoing off the trees. This time, no one fell for it.

"The police were searching for that wolf all day," Eddie said. "But they didn't find it. My stepfather got some calls from some of his buddies on the police force. They couldn't find any paw prints to track."

"Don't wolves travel in packs?" Callie said, tightening her jacket around her shoulders. "I seem to remember that from some science class."

Roxie frowned. "Hey, these woods are scary enough without a bunch of wolves hunting for meat."

Riley laughed and wrapped his big arms around her, almost smothering her. "The wolf won't want you, Roxie. You're too bony."

Danny grinned at Riley. "He'll have a feast on you, man. You'll be like Thanksgiving dinner."

We all laughed. Riley growled at Danny, an animal growl. Then he laughed, too.

"The wolves will be so busy with Riley, the rest of us can just stand and watch," Danny said.

The camping equipment had all been unloaded from Danny's SUV. Danny slammed the hatchback shut. "Are we really crazy to be doing this?" he asked, suddenly serious.

"There's no problem," Eddie said, stepping up to Danny. He had his hands in the pockets of his jacket. I caught a flash of excitement in his eyes.

"We'll all be safe," he said. "Trust me." His eyes moved from one of us to the next. I tried to read the strange smile on his face, but I couldn't.

"Can you keep a secret?" Eddie asked. "Seriously. Can you?"

Everyone muttered yes.

"Okay," Eddie said. "Here's why we'll be safe."

He removed his right hand from his jacket and pulled out a gun.

9.

We all stared at the gun in silence. Callie took several steps back until she bumped into the side of the SUV. Roxie grabbed Riley's hand. Danny stood frozen with his mouth open.

"Why'd you bring that?" I cried.

Eddie shrugged. "For protection. If that wolf shows, I'm going to be ready for it."

That was greeted with even more silence.

"Where'd you get it?" Riley demanded.

"It's my stepdad's," Eddie said, lowering the gun to his side. "It's a .38 snubnose revolver."

"H-he *gave* it to you?" Callie stammered.

Eddie shook his head. "No way. Lou doesn't know I know where he keeps his gun collection."

"I don't believe you, Eddie," Danny said, stepping up to him, his eyes down on the revolver. "I don't believe you brought that." He raised his eyes to Eddie's. "Is it loaded?"

A thin smile crossed Eddie's face. His eyes flashed. "Maybe."

Riley burst between Eddie and Danny. He made a grab for the gun. "Let me see that."

"No!" Callie screamed. "Put it away. Put it away or I'm leaving." She shoved Riley aside and brought her face up close to Eddie's. "I'm serious. Put it away, Eddie. I don't want to be on the news where one of us accidentally gets shot."

"She's right," Roxie chimed in. "Lose the gun, Eddie. Come on. You're going to spoil everything."

"Okay, okay." Eddie raised his hands in surrender. The revolver gleamed in the pale moonlight. He tucked it back into his jacket. "Just trying to be safe, you know. No big thing."

I breathed a sigh of relief. I think we all did. I suddenly realized I didn't know Eddie as well as I thought I did. I knew about his family struggling to make ends meet. I knew Eddie could be tough. I knew about his temper.

But I was surprised he was reckless enough to take one of his stepdad's guns and bring it into the woods for what was supposed to be a peaceful overnight adventure.

Eddie kept his eyes on me as we gathered up all the coolers and sleeping bags and equipment. I think he was looking for a sign of disapproval, looking to see if I was upset with him. I just rolled my eyes. I didn't want to start a whole thing with him.

Callie and Roxie led the way into the trees. They were

both talking at once, but I couldn't hear what they were talking about. Riley followed, carrying a portable tent on each shoulder. He liked to show off.

"Just don't shake the beer," he called back to Danny, who carried the case in front of his chest.

Danny groaned. He has skinny arms and isn't exactly a weight lifter. "Whose idea was this?" he demanded.

"Shut up. It was yours," Eddie told him. "Remember? You said we had to do something totally crazy before we graduate?"

"I meant like wearing our clothes backward to school or something," Danny muttered. He shifted the case of beer onto his shoulder. "I hate the woods. I hate nature."

Callie laughed. "You didn't say that when you begged me to come with you."

"I didn't *beg* you," Danny insisted. "I just asked—" But when he saw the rest of us all laughing at him, he didn't finish his sentence.

The moon grew brighter, and the tree leaves glimmered like silver under its light. The ground was wet from the evening dew. Everything around us sparkled. It was seriously beautiful, and I began to feel happy that I'd agreed to come.

We stopped in a small clearing of tall grass and set up the three tents in a triangle facing each other. The three boys went back to the trees to search for firewood so we could build a fire. It was a warm spring night but the air still felt tingly and cool.

"That moon pendant on your neck is glowing," Callie said.

I turned. I didn't realize she was standing next to me. I glanced down at the pendant. "It isn't glowing," I said. "It's just catching the moonlight."

Callie squinted at it. "Weird. I really thought it lit up."

"I had a big dinner, but I'm starving," Roxie said. "I think being outdoors makes me hungry. The air or something."

I squinted at her. She's as skinny as a ten-year-old. "A big dinner? What did you have? A meatball?"

Callie laughed but Roxie didn't.

"Not funny, Emmy. I eat a lot," Roxie insisted. "Seriously. It just doesn't show. I have a weird metabolism, I guess."

I kept gazing into the trees. I confess, I felt a little insecure without the guys around. The trees were still. There was no breeze at all. It was like the whole world was still. And for a moment, I thought this can't be real. I can't be here. This must be another dream.

A dumb thought. I forced it from my mind.

The guys returned with armloads of broken branches. They dumped them in the space between the three tents. Danny kept rubbing one hand. "Think I got a splinter."

"Man up," Riley said, giving him a shoulder block that almost sent him sprawling to the ground.

Eddie squatted down beside the pile of sticks. He pulled out a plastic lighter, clicked on a flame, and lowered it to the firewood. He raised his eyes to me. "Did you know I was a Boy Scout once? I got kicked out."

"Big surprise," Danny muttered.

"Why'd you get kicked out?" I asked.

"We were learning how to tie knots, and I tied another scout to a tree." Eddie shrugged. "I was just practicing. You know. But it turned into a big thing."

It took a few tries, but the fire finally caught. The twigs and sticks began to flame and crackle. Eddie climbed to his feet and stepped back. His face looked so serious and handsome in the shadowy red firelight.

"That fire is going to last about ten minutes," Danny said.

"So we'll get more wood," Riley said.

Roxie said something but I didn't hear her. Something in the trees at the edge of the clearing caught my eye. Something moved at the side of a tall evergreen shrub. Just a blur. But I recognized it.

"The wolf!" I cried, my voice tight, hoarse. "It's there. The wolf!"

"Everybody freeze!" Eddie shouted. He raised the revolver, aimed at the crouching figure beside the shrub, and fired it.

10.

The sound of the shot reverberated in my ears, like a sharp burst of thunder. I heard a squeal. Shrill and high. It lasted for only a second.

No one moved. I kept my eyes on the shrub across the clearing. I didn't see anything now. Nothing moved.

Without a word, all six of us took off, running hard, sliding and slipping on the tall, dew-wet grass. I ran breathlessly across the clearing, the grass bright now under the light from the crescent moon.

A few feet from the shrub, I skidded to a stop, breathing hard. I pressed my hands against my waist, struggling to catch my breath. And stared down at the raccoon Eddie had shot.

It lay on its back, its dark, ringed eyes wide open, its forepaws limp at its side. Its belly was bloodstained, a large hole ripped through the fur.

"A perfect shot," Riley said, poking at the dead creature with the toe of his shoe. "You hit the bull's-eye, Eddie. But that's the weirdest looking wolf I ever saw."

Danny laughed. Roxie and Callie hung back, huddled together. Eddie still had the pistol in his hand. He tucked it back in his jacket pocket and turned to me. "Did you really think it was a wolf?"

I nodded. I didn't know what to say. My thoughts were a jumble.

Danny stepped in front of Eddie, a grin on his face. "I know what we have to do now. Eddie, you have to bury this guy in the pet cemetery."

"Awesome," Riley chimed in. "We'll give it a name and make a tombstone for it."

"Or maybe we'll call it the Tomb of the Unknown Raccoon," Danny said.

"You're a grave digger now, right, Eddie? I mean, that's your job. Digging graves for animals? Cool job."

Eddie scowled at them. "You guys are so funny. Remind me to laugh later." He wasn't enjoying this. I knew what he was thinking. This was supposed to be a fun, romantic night in the woods. Why were these guys acting like jerks?

"I'm not joking," Danny insisted. "I really think we should bury it."

"Okay. *You* bury it," Eddie grunted. He stepped behind the dead raccoon and *kicked* it into the air. It made a squishy *thud* as it bounced off Danny's chest.

Danny let out a roar and rushed at Eddie. He tackled Eddie around the waist and drove him to the ground. Eddie swung a punch at Danny's chest and missed.

I rushed forward, intending to break it up. But Danny

was already laughing. He reached down and helped Eddie to his feet. Then he brushed the dirt off the legs of Eddie's jeans slapping it with both hands.

"Truce?" Danny said.

Eddie didn't reply, but I could see he was over it. The six of us walked back to our fire. Callie and Roxie said it was their turn to collect firewood. They disappeared into the trees.

Eddie and I got settled. We sat against the side of our tent. He slid his arm around my shoulders, and we kissed. I closed my eyes. I wanted the woods to disappear for a while. I wanted to close out everything but Eddie and me.

A popping sound made me jump. I recognized the sound. Riley popping open a can of beer. I snuggled against Eddie's cheek. I closed my eyes again and pressed my lips against his for a long kiss.

Angry voices interrupted. I turned, a little breathless, and saw Danny and Riley gesturing and shouting at each other. Roxie and Callie stood behind them with armloads of firewood.

"What is *this* fight about?" I cried. "What is your problem tonight?"

They didn't reply. Danny gave Riley a hard shove. But Riley is a mountain. He didn't budge.

"What are they fighting about?" I asked Eddie.

"I don't care," he said. He jumped up and pulled me to my feet. "Let's go." He grabbed both hands and gave me a hard tug.

"Huh?" I resisted. "Where are we going? We were just getting comfortable. You and I—"

"I've had it," Eddie growled. "All this fighting and stuff. Babies. Seriously." He pulled me again.

I followed him toward the trees. The moon disappeared again behind clouds, and we walked in total darkness. The air grew cooler as we stepped under the trees. A narrow dirt path curved through the woods, tangles of shrubs and prickly vines brushing us as we passed through.

"Eddie—stop," I said. "Where are we going? Where are you taking me?"

"You'll see," he said. He pushed a low tree limb away from the path.

I felt a sharp sting and swatted a mosquito off my forehead. Eddie was walking faster now, his head low, arms swinging at his sides. I hurried to catch up.

"Hey, Eddie—wait. Where are we going? Really."

He spun around, his face hidden in darkness. "Don't you trust me?"

I answered reluctantly. "Yes, of course, but . . ."

He took my hand and helped me over a fallen log. He kissed my cheek, then tugged me along the path. Something slithered over my foot. A snake?

A shiver ran down my back. I lowered my gaze. Too dark to see anything down there.

The trees ended, and we found ourselves in another clearing. Small and flat. Patchy weeds and low pine bushes.

Eddie kicked a stone out of our way. He stopped in front of a wide, old tree, the bark crusted with deep ruts.

"Here we are," he said, his eyes locked on mine.

"Here we are *where*?" I asked. "There's nothing here, Eddie. We're—"

He covered my mouth with a kiss. "This is our place, Emmy," he said quietly, lowering his hands around my waist and holding me. "This is our secret place."

I gazed around the small circle of weeds and low shrubs. *This is weird,* I thought. *Eddie isn't usually this emotional. Or, is it just that I don't know him very well?*

He held me close, staring into my eyes. I knew he was waiting for a response. But I was a little in shock, I guess.

"Do you like it?" he asked finally. "I scouted it out, Emmy. A secret place just for us."

Definitely weird. But sweet.

"I like it," I whispered.

Then I gasped as he pulled a knife from his jeans pocket.

He flipped open the blade and raised the knife. "I'm going to make it so this place will always be ours," he said.

11.

My heartbeats pattered in my chest. I pulled back, pulled free of his arms, and staggered a few steps away, my eyes on the knife blade.

First a gun. Then a knife. How dangerous is he?

Eddie wouldn't hurt me. Of course not.

To my surprise, Eddie swung away from me and raised the knife to the tree. I watched with my arms tightly wrapped around my waist. My breathing slowly returned to normal as he dug the blade into the soft trunk of the old tree and began to carve.

"Eddie—?" I called out. But he raised his free hand to silence me.

He rested his left hand on the trunk and carved with his right hand, the knife scratching away at the wood, small pieces of bark falling to the ground.

He didn't look back. He worked quickly, intently, bringing his face close to the tree. Finally, he lowered the knife and stepped back. When he turned to me, he had a smile on his face.

The moon reappeared and a shaft of pale light fell over his work. I took a step forward and saw what he had carved. *Eddie ♥ Emmy.*

"Sweet," I said.

He brushed away some chips of bark with his fingers and stood admiring his own work. "Our special place," he murmured.

I stepped up and squeezed his hand. "Hope you didn't hurt the tree."

He snickered. "It's like a tattoo. A tree tattoo. It only hurts for a little while."

"Eddie, do you have a tattoo?" I realized again how little I knew about him.

He didn't answer. He looked away from me and tapped the knife blade on the rough bark below his carving. "Hey."

"What's wrong?" I said. "Shouldn't we be getting back to the others?"

Something caught my eye at the edge of the small clearing. I squinted into the silvery light. A rabbit. A scrawny rabbit, standing still as a statue on its hind legs. Ears straight up. Tiny dark eyes locked on us.

Eddie tapped the tree trunk rapidly with the knife blade. "Weird," he muttered. He jabbed the blade into the soft bark.

Then he slid one hand to the other side of the trunk. I

saw a dark hole there, a hole in the trunk nearly as big as a soccer ball.

"Whoa. This tree is hollow," Eddie said, his face twisted in surprise.

"Hollow? Really?"

He nodded and shoved his hand into the hole. "Hey. How weird is this? Emmy—there's something in here."

I stepped up beside him. "Inside the tree trunk? What is it?"

He pulled his arm back. Jerked it hard a few times, trying to free whatever was gripped in his hand, struggling to pry it from the opening. Finally, he gave a hard tug and staggered back.

I stared at the leather briefcase in his hand. Eddie raised it into the light. "Oh, wow. Oh, wow. I don't believe this," he said. "What is *this* doing in there?"

12.

Moonlight caught the briefcase and made the dark leather glow. I could see there wasn't a scratch on it or any wear and tear. It was like new.

Eddie twirled it in his hand by the handle. "How did this get in the tree?" he asked.

I didn't have an answer. He dropped to his knees and worked the latch on the briefcase's front. His fingers fumbled at it for a few seconds. Then I heard it click, and Eddie pulled the latch open.

He lowered his head and spread the satchel open. "Oh, wow. Wow." He kept murmuring to himself.

"What is it?" I asked. "What's in there?" I dropped to my knees beside him.

He reached inside and pulled up a stack of paper. No. Not paper. As my eyes focused, I realized he held a thick stack of money.

He dropped it back into the briefcase and pulled out another stack. His eyes were wide with shock and excitement.

His hands trembled as he shuffled through the bills, examining them.

"All hundreds," he said finally. "Emmy, all hundreds. Look. Look at this." He pulled up a huge handful.

I took them from him and spread them in my hands like a deck of cards.

"Ohmigod. Ohmigod, Eddie."

"Thousands of dollars," Eddie said in a whisper. He tilted the case toward me. I could see that it was jammed to the top with money.

"There's thousands of dollars in here. All hundreds," he said. He swallowed hard. He kept blinking rapidly, in disbelief, I guessed.

My heart was pounding in my chest. "Put it back," I said.

He gasped, as if I had said something shocking. "Huh?"

"Put it back, Eddie," I urged. "Whoever left it there . . . whoever hid it . . . well . . . we don't want to get involved."

"Are you crazy?" His words came out shrill, his voice high. "This is unbelievable, Emmy. This is a miracle. This money . . . it will solve all my family's problems."

I grabbed his arm and squeezed it. "Listen to me. Why would someone hide this money? I mean, maybe it's stolen. Or maybe it's drug money somebody had to stash away."

He trained his strange gray eyes on me. "So?"

"They'll come back for it. They won't be good people," I said, my voice trembling. "Think about it, Eddie. They might be really bad people. And whoever it is, they'll come back for it.

"Did you ever hear of finders keepers?" he said. He moved the briefcase, swinging it out of my reach.

"Don't be crazy," I said. "Please. Don't be crazy. You're not thinking clearly. Whoever it is will come looking for the money. You don't want to get involved."

"They won't have a clue who took it," Eddie said, latching the case. "How would they know? Check for fingerprints on the tree trunk?" He laughed, a crazy laugh.

"Not funny," I said. "This is too dangerous."

Suddenly, I felt a sharp tingle at the back of my neck. My senses went alert.

Is someone watching us?

I spun around and squinted across the clearing. Was it the rabbit? No. The rabbit was gone. But the feeling lingered, just a strong hunch that we were being watched.

I climbed to my feet. My knees were wet from the grass beneath the tree. "Eddie, I'm begging you. Put the money back."

"You're no fun," he said. "I thought you were a fun person."

I let out an exasperated sigh. "This isn't about fun. This is about taking someone's money and getting into incredible danger."

"I-I need this money," he stammered. "My family . . ."

"And what about the others?" I cried, motioning toward the campfire. "We have to tell the others about this, don't we?"

He shook his head. "No way." He climbed to his feet,

gripping the case tightly in his right hand. "It's ours, Emmy. It's our secret. We don't want to split it six ways—*do* we?"

Before I could answer, a voice cried out: "Hey—what have you got there?"

Eddie and I spun around. I saw Riley first, hands on his waist, his eyes on the case. Danny, Roxie, and Callie came trotting up behind him.

"Emmy, we didn't know where you two went," Callie said. "We thought—"

"What's in the briefcase?" Riley repeated. "Where'd you get that?"

Eddie hesitated. I saw him grip the case handle tighter.

"Who brings a briefcase to a campout?" Danny demanded. "What's going down here? Why do you two look so weirded out?"

"It's . . . kind of a long story," I said.

Eddie nodded. "I found this," he said, raising the case in front of him. "In this tree." He slapped the trunk. It made a hollow *thud*.

"You found a briefcase in a tree?" Danny scrunched his face up, squinting at Eddie. "Seriously?"

"What's this *really* about?" Roxie demanded, turning to me. "Why are you acting so strange? What's up with all the suspense? Why did you two sneak off in the first place?"

"Eddie's telling the truth," I said. "We found it in this tree. Let's go back to the campsite and relax," I said. "Eddie and I will tell you all about it. I swear."

And that's what we did. We settled in front of the fire.

Riley popped open a few more beers. I took one, too. I felt so jittery and tense, I thought it might help calm me.

Eddie opened the case and showed everyone the stacks and stacks of hundred-dollar bills. "There's got to be a hundred thousand dollars in here," he said.

Danny slapped his forehead. He jumped to his feet and did a wild dance. "We're rich! We're totally rich!" He and Riley bumped fists.

Then Riley tilted back his beer can and emptied it in one gulp. He crushed it and heaved the can against a tree. Then he joined Riley and Eddie and they bopped around like lunatics, laughing and shouting.

I saw that Callie and Roxie had grown very quiet. They didn't dance or laugh or cry out or join the celebration in any way.

When the boys finally settled back down to the ground, the argument began. Callie spoke first, softly, timidly. "We have to take it to the police. You're not really thinking of keeping it—are you?"

"Of *course* we're keeping it!" Danny cried. "We can divide it up tonight. The money goes six different ways—and then who will be able to find it? No one."

Eddie frowned. "Divide it up tonight? Well . . ."

"What's wrong with that?" Danny's tone suddenly turned angry, challenging. "You want to keep it for yourself?"

"No way," Eddie said. "For sure, we'll share it. But . . ."

"We have to be careful," I said. "I mean, this much money . . . it could be really dangerous to keep it. We don't know who hid it in the tree. We don't want to put ourselves in horrible danger."

Callie stood up. Her legs were trembling and she had both hands down at her sides curled into tight fists. "We can't argue about this," she said through gritted teeth. "Why are we even talking about it? We have to turn it over to the police. It *has* to be stolen money. Maybe there was a bank robbery or something. And we—"

"There wasn't any bank robbery in Shadyside," Eddie told her. "You know my stepdad is a cop. If there was a bank robbery, trust me, he'd be talking about it. He'd be talking about it day and night."

"Then where did the money come from?" Roxie demanded. "Look at that case. It's fresh. It wasn't in that tree for long. Someone just put it in there. And they'll be coming back for it real soon."

"That's why we've got to split it up right away," Danny said. He turned to Riley. "You agree?"

Riley shrugged. "I'll take my share now. No problem." He laughed.

"Don't be stupid," Eddie said, latching the case. "We have to hide the money till we know it's safe to spend it."

"He's right," I said. "What if it's marked money? You know. Like in a bank robbery. And we start spending it, and we're caught. And then they think *we're* the ones who stole it."

Callie was still tensely on her feet, her body rigid, her

fists tight. "Whoever hid that money is guilty of something bad. It has to be from some crime. We can't take the risk. The police will be looking for it. We have to take it to them—right now." She shuddered. "What if the person who planted the briefcase is still in the woods?"

Those words sent a chill down my back.

"You all can argue all night," Danny said, shaking his head. "I'll take my share now." He dove forward and grabbed the briefcase out of Eddie's hand.

Eddie uttered an angry cry and grabbed Danny by the shoulders. He shook Danny hard, and the case fell to the ground.

Eddie gave Danny a hard shove, sending him tumbling backward. Danny stopped himself before he fell into the campfire.

"Whoa!" Riley cried. "Whoa!" He tried to block Danny from charging back at Eddie. But Danny swerved around him. He tackled Eddie around the knees. Eddie fell to the ground. Scrambled to his knees. Made a grab for the briefcase.

Danny kicked it out of Eddie's reach. Eddie dove for it.

And I screamed as I saw the revolver fall from Eddie's jacket pocket.

Both boys saw it, too. Danny dropped to his knees and stretched his hand toward it. But Eddie got there first.

I saw Danny's hand wrap around Eddie's. They were both grunting and groaning. They looked like two arm wrestlers, struggling and straining, their hands closed over the gun.

I screamed again, a shrill scream of horror, as the gun exploded. The sound of the shot echoed off the trees all around.

My scream cut off. I started to choke.

I watched Danny grab his stomach and crumple to the ground.

"You killed him!" Callie's scream throbbed in my ears. "You killed him! You killed him!"

13.

Still screaming, Callie ran to Danny and dropped beside him.

Danny raised his head slowly. He gazed around, his eyes unfocused, as if he was dazed.

"Danny? Danny?" Callie cried, reaching for him.

He sat up. "I'm okay." He ran his hands down his chest, then his legs. "The shot—it frightened me. I just dropped. Reflexes, I guess."

Callie held onto him, hugging his shoulders. "You're not shot?"

Danny shook his head. "I felt the bullet whiz past me. Like a burst of air. And the sound—" He covered his ears with both hands.

Eddie moved quickly and lowered a hand to help Danny up. The rest of us stood in place. No one spoke.

Eddie tucked the gun into his jacket pocket. Then he stood Danny up and brushed him off. His way of apologizing, I guess

"Sorry about that," he said finally, his eyes on the ground. "It was an accident. You know that, right?"

Danny nodded. "We were both being stupid," he murmured.

"Maybe this will bring you guys to your senses," Roxie said.

"I'll second that," I chimed in. "Okay. We found some money. We can't fight about it. We have to stay calm and figure out the best thing to do."

"Everyone knows the best thing to do," Callie said, still on the ground. "But no one wants to do that."

"You mean turn it over to the police?" I said.

She nodded.

"That's crazy—" Eddie started.

But I held a hand up to silence him. "Let's not start fighting again. Let's vote. Settle it right away."

"I vote that we take the money and we all buy new Corvettes," Riley said. "We have a Corvette Club, all six of us, and we meet every week and go roaring around together, terrifying everyone in town."

"Shut up, Riley," Roxie said.

He pretended to be hurt. "Come on. It's a plan—isn't it?"

Riley's uncle once showed up in a new red Corvette and took Riley for a ride in it, and he's been obsessed with Corvettes ever since. He draws them and puts together plastic model Corvettes. He even made his parents take him to the Corvette factory in Kentucky one summer so he could watch them being made.

"Are we going to vote or not?" Callie demanded, ignoring Riley's suggestion.

"Okay," I said. "How many want to take the bag of money to the police?"

Callie and I raised our hands. No one else.

Eddie laughed. "You're outnumbered. So . . . now what? I say we hide the money in some safe place till we know more about it."

Danny eyed Eddie suspiciously. "And *you* get to choose the safe place?"

"Stop it, Danny," I said. "We're starting over, remember. We have to keep the secret, all six of us. And we have to trust each other. We're friends, right?"

"Sure, we're friends," Danny said. "But we never had thousands of dollars before."

"And you think that could mess up our friendship?" Eddie demanded.

Danny backed away. "I just meant someone might be tempted to . . . you know . . . maybe take some of it. I mean, no one here is rich. We've all got money problems, right? I just want to know who makes the rules, here? Is it you, Eddie?"

"I guess," Eddie said. "I'm the one who found the money. I think—"

"But we're going to split it equally, right, Eddie?" I broke in. I could see Danny was ready to fight again. "All six of us share the secret, and all six of us get the same share. And we all have a say about things."

"For sure," Eddie said.

Danny relaxed. He helped Callie to her feet and slid his arm around her waist.

"So we're definitely going to hide it somewhere?" Roxie asked.

"Just to be safe," Eddie said. He raised the briefcase and unlatched it. "Hey, how about this? A symbol of good faith." He reached in and pulled out a stack of bills.

I grabbed his arm. "Eddie? What are you doing?"

"I told you. A symbol of good faith." He counted out six hundred-dollar bills and handed one to each of us. He jammed one into his jeans pocket. Then he latched the briefcase shut.

Roxie raised the money close to her face, holding it in both hands. "Wow. I never held a hundred-dollar bill before. Hard to believe it's real."

Callie shook her head. "I just want to go on record," she said, folding the bill in her hand. "If something bad happens because of this, I warned everyone."

"Relax, Callie," I said. "Seriously. Just chill. Nothing bad is going to happen."

Whoa. Was *I* wrong.

14.

Eddie said he knew the perfect place to hide the money. So we piled into Danny's SUV, and Eddie directed us to the pet cemetery outside Martinsville where he works. It was late, nearly midnight, and there were few cars on the road.

About a mile from Martinsville, a deer leaped out onto the highway in front of us. The headlights lit it up—so bright I could see the startled look in the animal's eyes. Danny hit the brake and swerved hard, making us all scream.

My hand squeezed the arm of the door so hard, it throbbed with pain. I forced myself to breathe. I let out a cry as the deer managed to scamper to the other side.

"What a boring night!" Riley joked. We all laughed. Tense laughter.

I sat next to Callie, and I could feel the fear and tension coming off her. She clasped her hands tightly together in her lap. And she kept her eyes straight ahead, focused on the road in the darting headlights.

I wanted to say something to make her feel better. It always makes me uncomfortable to be with someone who is unhappy. I'm not a rah-rah cheerleader type. But I like people to be happy. But as I said, I don't know Callie very well at all. So I didn't know what to say to her.

Danny slowed the car as the tall main gate and the sign PET HEAVEN filled the windshield. Eddie directed him to the side of the wide cemetery lot. He jumped out of the passenger seat, the briefcase gripped tightly in his hand.

Snakes of cloud floated over the pale crescent moon. The old trees that dotted the grounds stood still as death, black against the purple night sky.

We followed Eddie into the cemetery, our shoes sinking into the soft dirt. Once again, I felt a chill at the back of my neck, felt all my senses go alert.

Something evil here . . .

Why did I keep having that frightening feeling? Was it just because this was a cemetery? Because the decaying corpses of dozens of dogs and cats were lying under our feet?

Roxie brushed up against my side. "This is way creepy," she said in a voice just above a whisper.

I nodded. I pointed to a tall gravestone. In the dim light, we both read the inscription: HARRY. 2004–2016. MY BEST FRIEND. WE'LL GO FOR WALKS IN HEAVEN.

Roxie shuddered. "That gravestone probably cost big bucks, right?"

"Probably," I said. "People love their pets." But I wasn't

thinking about the gravestone. I was thinking about how I had such a feeling of dread every time I came here.

Roxie twisted her face in disgust. "Ooh. What's that rotten smell?"

I shrugged. "Beats me." I held my breath. The odor really was totally putrid.

Eddie led us along a narrow, rutted path between two rows of graves. A few of the gravestones were draped with wilting flowers. One of the stones had a color photo of a German Shepherd printed on its front.

I brushed back my hair and wiped away drops of sweat from my forehead. It was a warm night, and there was no air here at all, not the tiniest breeze. As if the whole world was still and dead.

Toward the back of the cemetery, I saw a yellow light. I stared hard and realized it was the office building. The light was on in the front. Was Mac Stanton awake? Could he see us from there?

I stepped away from Roxie, eager to ask Eddie about the light in the office. "Mac can't see anything from there," Eddie said. "We're too far away, and it's too dark."

He stopped at an open grave, dirt piled in a low mound at one end. The grave was about three feet deep. A shovel lay on its side beyond the mound of dirt.

Eddie turned and waited for the others to catch up. "This is perfect."

Danny stepped up beside him. "You're going to bury the briefcase in this grave?"

Eddie nodded. "Yeah. It won't take long to cover it up. We'll bury it here, then come back as soon as we know it's safe."

"Better be soon," Riley muttered. "I haven't found a summer job."

"Yeah," Roxie chimed in. "That hundred dollars you gave us isn't going to go far."

Callie remained silent, her arms crossed in front of her. She hadn't said a word the whole drive to the cemetery.

"We'll come back and get it as soon as we know no one is looking for it," Eddie said. "You know I work here. So I'll be able to keep an eye on it."

"That's what I'm *afraid* of," Danny said. "*You* keeping an eye on it."

"Give it a rest, Danny," I said. "We said we're going to trust each other, remember? Stop trying to start fights."

He raised both hands and put this innocent, wide-eyed expression on his face.

"Eddie isn't going anywhere," I told him. "He isn't going to take the money and fly off to the Bahamas."

"Not a bad idea," Riley joked. No one laughed.

"If you have a problem, you'll know where to find him," I told Danny. "So stop trying—"

I felt my phone buzz in my pocket. Who would call me after midnight?

I tugged it out and raised the screen to my face. Then I tapped to accept the call. "Sophie? What's wrong?" I asked.

"Emmy? Where are you?" Her voice sounded tiny, frightened. "Where are you?"

Panic tightened my throat. I had to think fast. No way I could tell her where I was. "I'm . . . uh . . . with my friends. Why? What's wrong, Sophie? Is something wrong?"

"I . . . sorry . . . sorry to bother you, but . . ."

"Sophie? Are you home? Is everyone okay?" My voice cracked on the word *okay*.

"Yeah. Fine," she answered hesitantly. "I . . . was walking home from the library. I stopped at Lefty's. You know. To see if there was anyone I know there. But the place was almost empty, and I really wasn't hungry . . ."

"And? Why are you telling me this?" I demanded.

I looked up and saw the others watching me. I turned and walked a few steps down the path between the gravestones. Behind me, I could hear Eddie shoveling the dirt onto the grave.

"I think I saw it," Sophie said. "Emmy, I think I saw it. The wolf."

I gasped. "Huh? You saw it? Where? Where were you?"

"Walking home. By the Malcolms' house. You know. Across from the playground."

"The wolf was on the playground?"

"It was watching me, Emmy. It stood with its head down, and its back arched. I could see the black fur raised on its back. It followed me with its eyes. Incredible blue eyes."

No! Could it really be the wolf from my dreams?

"What did you do, Sophie? Did you run?"

"No. I couldn't. I was too afraid. I just stared back at it. And after a while, it slinked away."

I suddenly felt strange. Sophie's voice seemed to fade until she seemed far away. She was still talking, but her words didn't make sense to me. I gasped as the dark trees all around appeared to lean toward me.

That's impossible. The trees aren't moving. What's wrong with me?

"Emmy? Are you still there?" Sophie's voice a mile away.

The trees tilted toward me, reaching for me. The ground starting to tilt and sway. The sky rocking. The crescent moon sliding to and fro . . . trembling as if it was about to fall from the sky.

So dizzy . . . why do I feel so dizzy?

"Emmy? Are you coming home? Where are you? Please come home. It isn't safe, Emmy. It isn't safe out there."

Sophie's voice sounded so distant. Like a million miles away.

I tilted my head back, raised my face to the shimmering moon, and suddenly had such a powerful urge . . . an urge to open my mouth . . . to open my soul . . . and to howl, howl like a wolf, howl out all the wildness inside me . . . howl and howl and never stop.

15.

Someone grabbed my arm. Callie. Her eyes were wide with alarm. "Emmy? Are you okay?"

I blinked at her. It took me a while to realize my mouth hung wide open. I closed it, breathing hard, my chest fluttery, blinking more, struggling to make her come into focus.

"Emmy? What's wrong?" She held onto my arm.

"Nothing," I managed to say. "I'm okay."

Her pale green eyes studied me. "You had the weirdest look on your face. Like you were going to faint or something." I saw that the others were staring at me, too.

"That phone call," Callie said. "Did you get bad news?"

"No . . . I . . ." I didn't know how to answer her. Glancing down, I realized I still had the phone gripped tightly in my hand.

I pressed it to my ear. "Sophie? Are you still there? Sophie?"

Silence.

"My sister," I told them, tucking the phone into my jeans. "She thinks she saw the wolf. She got totally freaked."

"The wolf? Really?" Roxie stepped over to me. "Where'd she see it?"

"A few blocks from our house." I raised my eyes to the trees. They didn't appear to be leaning toward me anymore. But my vision was still cloudy, my skin tingled, and my dizziness lingered. "I think I have to get home," I said. "Sophie sounded pretty bad."

Eddie tossed a shovelful of dirt into the grave. He gazed at me. "Aren't your parents home? Can't they take care of her?" I could see the disappointment on his face. He probably wanted to go back to our campsite in the woods for the night.

But I was no longer in the mood. And watching the faces around the grave, I didn't think anyone else was, either.

"My parents are useless in an emergency," I said. "They just tell us to calm down and not be drama queens. No matter what." I was telling the truth.

"My mom just passes out the Xanax," Roxie said. "She thinks it's the cure for everything."

"I'm almost finished here," Eddie said, tossing more dirt on the grave. "I can ride with you." He glanced around the group. We were all standing very still, watching his work. "Hey, thanks for pitching in, everyone," he grumbled.

"Cut us some slack," Riley said. "There was only one shovel."

I noticed that Danny had gotten very quiet. I saw his eyes follow the shovel as Eddie smoothed the dirt over the grave. I wondered what he was thinking. After a few seconds, he saw me watching him, and he turned abruptly toward the trees.

Eddie tossed the shovel onto the ground. He wiped his hands on the legs of his jeans. "Let's roll," he said.

The lights were still on in the office at the back of the cemetery. Squinting hard, I thought I saw a shadow move in the front window. But I was too far away to see clearly.

Eddie slid a hand onto my shoulder as we walked toward the car. "You okay?"

I nodded. "Worried about Sophie."

Worried about Sophie and about me.

"What a boring night!" Riley exclaimed. That made us all laugh.

"Hey, we're almost rich," Eddie said.

"Almost," Danny repeated. I could hear the bitterness in his voice. I hoped he wasn't going to cause more trouble.

Sophie was waiting up for me in our room. Her face was sweaty even though a breeze was floating in through the open window, making the curtains dance.

She sat up on her knees on her bed as I came in. Her nightshirt was caught beneath her legs. She tugged it free.

I turned on the ceiling light. Sophie's cheeks were flushed. Her normally perfect black hair was matted to one side on her head. "I didn't know if you'd come home or not," she said softly, her eyes studying me.

"I was worried about you. You sounded so weird," I said.

"You weren't at Rachel Martin's," Sophie said, frowning. "I tried her house first."

"You *what*?" I returned her stare. "Why didn't you just call my cell? You knew I wasn't at Rachel's. So you were checking up on me? Why?"

She stuck her chin out. "Mom and Dad think you're so perfect, and I know you're not."

I groaned. "Sophie, please don't start this. It's been a long night—"

"Look at your sneakers," she said, ignoring me. "They're caked with mud. Where were you, Emmy? Where were you really?"

"I'm sick of you being jealous all the time," I snapped. I didn't mean to say it. It just burst out. Now that I'd started, I couldn't stop. "Sick of you checking up on me, watching me, commenting on everything, always criticizing me, always being angry. Poor Sophie. Poor Sophie. She's not as popular . . . not as much fun as Emmy. I'm sick of it! I've got my own problems, you know?"

Sophie's eyes went wide. She wasn't expecting such an explosion. She raised a finger to her lips."You're going to wake up Mom and Dad," she said.

"I don't care," I said.

"You just don't want to be honest with me," she said, her chin trembling, like she was getting ready to cry. "You don't think you can confide in me. Because you think I'm some kind of lower life form. I'm just some kind of larvae, or . . . no . . . a leech . . . some annoying creature you have to pull off your leg."

Huh? That made me burst out laughing.

After a few seconds, Sophie began to laugh, too. It was such an insane, dopey thing to say. We hadn't laughed together like that in a long time. We both laughed till we had tears in our eyes.

I dropped down on the edge of her bed and took her hand. "Okay," I said. "Okay, leech. How about a truce? What do you say?"

She wiped her eyes with her fingers. "Truce?"

"I'll tell you the truth," I said, "if you swear not to tell anyone. Can you keep a secret?"

I could see she was thinking about it. "Okay," she said finally. "Truce." We bumped knuckles.

So I told her the truth. Actually, it felt good to tell her. "I was with Eddie and a bunch of friends," I said. "We had this plan to camp out all night in the Fear Street Woods."

"Oh, wow," Sophie said. I could see the surprise on her face. "You and Eddie? You haven't even been going with him that long. I hope you were careful."

"It wasn't like that," I told her. "Eddie has this thing about camping . . . being outdoors. He says we spend too much time cramped up indoors. He says he can't breathe indoors. So he came up with the idea. And . . . we all thought it would be an adventure."

No way I planned to tell Sophie about the briefcase of money or burying it in the pet cemetery. I wasn't used to confiding in her. I decided I'd better go slow. See if she could be trusted. This was a good test. If she went running to my parents with this info, I'd know for sure that I couldn't trust her with any secrets.

"So . . . what happened?" Sophie asked, settling her back against the wall, straightening the hem of her nightshirt. "Why'd you come home?"

"Because of your call," I said. It wasn't a total lie. "You sounded so frightened and . . ." My voice trailed off. I suddenly remembered what happened to me after Sophie called. The whole world fading away . . . becoming a blur . . . and the overwhelming animal urge to howl.

Sophie's blue eyes locked on mine. "So I spoiled your night?"

"No. No way," I said. "It wasn't a good plan. The others weren't in the mood and . . . and I came home. We all went home." I stood up. I started to pace back and forth between our two beds. "So you'll keep my secret?"

"Of course," she said.

"Change of subject," I said. I had to ask her. I had to learn more. I couldn't stop thinking about my strange wolf dreams . . . the weird feelings I kept having. I wondered if Sophie could help me.

She straightened her legs over the bed, stuck out her arms, and leaning forward, stretched her hands over her bare feet. Sophie runs track, and she's also on the tennis team. She's an athlete. Something I'm not. And she's always stretching. Keeping loose. Testing her body.

I stopped pacing and stood over her. "Sophie, do you remember anything at all about when we flew to Prague when we were little and visited Great Aunt Marta?"

She stopped stretching. She narrowed her eyes at me. "That again?"

I nodded. "Yes. I know you told Mom you couldn't remember anything. But—"

"Hmmmmmm." Sophie scrunched her face up and shut her eyes. She does that when she's thinking hard about something. "Well . . ." She opened her eyes. "All I remember is that Aunt Marta was nearly blind, and she liked you better than me—even though she had trouble telling us apart."

Sophie smiled. "And I remember those weird little pies she made that tasted like sour meat and were totally gross."

I crossed my arms in front of me. "So you *do* remember a little bit."

"Well . . ."

"Do you remember anything about me being bitten by an animal? A dog or something that jumped out of the woods and attacked me?"

Sophie scrunched up her face again. "No. Not really. I don't remember that. Was I there when it happened?"

"I don't know," I said. "I can't remember it, either. But mom swears it happened."

"Was Mom there?" Sophie asked.

"No. Aunt Marta told her about it. Mom was visiting someone in the next town when it happened. But wouldn't I remember something as frightening as that?"

Sophie shrugged. "Emmy, are you coming to watch my track meet Monday after school? Mom and Dad can't make it."

"I'm really sorry. I can't either," I told her. "I have to pick up Eddie after his job. And then I'm having dinner at his house."

"But you *promised.*" Sophie's voice became shrill. She pounded the bedspread with both fists. "You promised you'd come, Emmy."

"I wish I could," I said. "Really. I—"

"How come I always come last?" Sophie demanded.

"Hey, I thought we had a truce," I said. "I'm sorry. I really am."

Sure, I felt guilty. I had promised to come. Sophie's track meets were very important to her. It was the only thing she was into, except for hanging out at the library and reading and studying all the time.

But then Eddie needed me to pick him up. And invited me to dinner.

I knew I should support Sophie more. But what could I do? I had a busy life. I had a boyfriend. I mean, I had friends to see and my own stuff to do after school. And frankly, track meets are way boring. Waiting two hours to watch your sister run in a thirty-second race? Yawn.

So, I apologized to Sophie a dozen more times. But she

wouldn't remove her pouty face. She turned to the wall and pulled the covers up over her head.

I got undressed quickly, pulled on a wrinkled-up pair of pajamas I'd stuffed in a dresser drawer, turned off the light, and climbed into my bed across the room.

It took a while to get to sleep. I kept running the scenes of the evening over and over in my head, like one of those six-second Vines that just won't stop. The campfire . . . the gun . . . our names carved on the tree . . . the brown leather briefcase of money . . .

When I finally fell asleep, I had another wolf dream.

In this dream, I was in a house I didn't recognize. In a brightly lit living room filled with red furniture. Everything red. I felt puzzled. Where was I? How did I get there?

In the dream, I wanted to figure everything out. I was frightened by my confusion. But before I could get clear on anything, I saw the wolf across the room.

Tall and powerful-looking, standing stiff and alert. The black wolf, gazing at me with those intelligent blue eyes. Ears straight up, jaw open just enough to reveal yellow, curled teeth.

My confusion gave way to fear. A terrifying staring match, the wolf and I. Neither of us blinked. Neither of us moved a muscle.

Studying each other. Testing each other.

And then suddenly, in my sleep, in my dream, I'm asking myself a frightening question:

Is the wolf watching me? Or am I the wolf?

16.

When I picked up Eddie at the pet cemetery the next afternoon, Mac Stanton stood with him near the gate. Mac had a white paper shopping bag in one hand and was shaking it in front of Eddie.

"Do you believe this?" Mac greeted me. "People dump their dead dogs over the fence in the middle of the night and expect me to take care of them."

Something thumped heavily in the bag as Mac shook it. I assumed it was a dead dog.

"That's terrible," I said. I didn't know what else to say. I could see that Mac was really angry.

"Do you know what the rent on this property is?" he demanded. He didn't expect an answer. He was just ranting. "It's sky high. So why do these idiots think I'm going to bury their dogs for nothing?"

I glanced at Eddie. He looked embarrassed.

"People are upset when their pet dies," I said. "I guess they're just not thinking clearly at the time."

Mac scowled at me. His gold tooth caught the sunlight. His face was bright red. "Well, *I'm* thinking clearly. I'll tell you that." He pointed up to a tree limb overhanging a row of graves. "See that? That's a security camera. I put them up all over the grounds. Next time someone comes in here at night to dump a dead dog, I'll know who it is."

He gazed up at the camera. "And don't think I won't come after them."

Swinging the shopping bag at his side, he spun around and stormed toward the office.

I stepped close to Eddie. "Wow. Is he always like this?" I whispered.

Mac slammed the office door behind him.

"He has a temper," Eddie said, shaking his head. "Sometimes he's a little out-of-control. But then a few seconds later, he's his usual grouchy self."

We both laughed. We climbed into the car, and I drove toward Eddie's house in the Old Village. It was a hot day, hazy and wet, the kind of day that made your skin prickle at the back of your neck, made you wish you were at the beach.

The air-conditioner in Mom's Corolla always takes twenty minutes to get cold. I smelled something sour, like rotted meat.

Eddie saw me sniffing the air. "It's me," he said. "The smell from the cemetery, it sticks to my clothes . . . to my skin. I can't figure out why it smells so bad there."

"Is it the crematorium?" I asked, turning onto Village Road.

"I don't think so," Eddie said. "Mac hasn't fried any animals since I've been working there."

I stopped for a light. My phone buzzed and vibrated. I pulled it out and gazed at the screen. A text from Sophie: "Finished second. Thanks for your support."

"What's that?" Eddie asked.

"My sister being bitter," I said. I tucked the phone back into my bag. "Sophie's feeling neglected these days."

"How come?" he asked.

"Because I've been neglecting her?"

We both laughed again. But I cut my laughter short. "She's going through a hard time. I'm not really sure why. We don't confide in each other a lot."

Eddie nodded. Traffic was moving slowly. Cars always got backed up around the Division Street Mall. Passing the mall made me think of some tees I wanted to buy at the Old Navy store. And that made me think about money. And *that* made me think about the briefcase full of money.

"Did Mac notice the filled-in grave?" I asked.

Eddie blinked. My question caught him by surprise. He shook his head. "No. He walked right past the grave. He was so steamed about the dog being heaved over the fence, he didn't notice anything."

"So you really think the money is safe there?"

"Sure," he said. "There are a bunch of recently dug

graves. Mac won't notice anything." He swept a hand back through his dark hair. "It'll be safe there. But I'd love to dig it up and hand everyone their shares."

I shivered. It was one thing to see all that money and bury it at night. It was all kind of dreamlike. It was definitely the kind of thing that would happen in a dream.

But talking about it in the daylight made it seem so much more real.

And so much more scary.

"I Googled *bank robbery in Shadyside,*" Eddie said. "But nothing came up. As soon as we know for sure where the money came from. . . ."

"I won't be able to keep it a secret from my parents," I said, shielding my eyes from the low sun that filled the windshield. "I mean, once I have my share. Thousands of dollars. I'll have to tell them about it. But how? How can I explain it?"

Eddie smiled and patted my hand. "Let's worry about that when the time comes. We can tell them you won the big bingo prize at the school fair."

"Not funny," I said.

"Hey, one step at a time, Emmy. When it's safe to take the money, we'll figure out a way to tell our parents. Do you really think they'll be shocked and horrified and want to turn it in to the police immediately?"

"I don't know. I—"

"I'll tell you one thing," Eddie said. "My stepdad will grab it up. He'll be thrilled. Sure, Lou is a cop. But he won't care where it came from. We need the money so bad . . . he'll be dancing on the dining room table, tossing it up in the air like confetti."

"Not sure about my parents," I said softly. I couldn't get rid of the heavy feeling of dread in the pit of my stomach. I wished I could have Eddie's confidence. He was so good at never letting anything get in his way. He just always seemed to be in control, ready to face anything.

"I think we can trust the others to keep the secret for now," Eddie said. He wasn't really talking to me now. He was thinking out loud. "I was worried about Danny. If anyone decided to dig up the briefcase and take his share of the money, it would be Danny. But I don't think . . ."

"Danny can be a jerk," I said. "And he loves to fight. But he would never do a thing like that."

Eddie remained silent, thinking about that, I guess.

I found a parking spot half a block from Eddie's house and squeezed into it. The houses are small and close together in the Old Village, and there are no driveways, so there's always a scramble for parking on the street.

We climbed out of the car, and I locked the doors. This isn't the best neighborhood in town. The sidewalk was cracked and rutted with weeds growing through the cracks. We walked along the curb. I wondered what Eddie's parents were like. I'd never met them. Never seen them at any school events.

"Mom's very quiet," Eddie said, as if reading my thoughts. "She doesn't say much, and she waits on Lou hand and foot. But she's the real boss of the family. When she has a strong opinion, Lou gripes and mutters, but he always backs down."

"And is he the tough-cop type?" I asked.

"Not really," Eddie said. We crossed the street. The house on the corner had its front window boarded up. "Lou likes to talk tough. But he isn't a bad guy. He used to take my brother Johnny and me hiking and fishing all the time, before Johnny went into the army. We had good times. Lou's favorite thing is to lie on the couch and watch sports on TV. He doesn't care what the sport is. It doesn't matter. He always falls asleep after about twenty minutes."

We started up the concrete steps to Eddie's house. It was a narrow gray shingle house with black shutters. The paint was peeling on some of the shutters, and one rain gutter was tilting off the roof at the side of the house.

"Of course, Lou's been totally depressed since he was suspended," Eddie said, lowering his voice as we crossed the front stoop. "Depressed and angry."

I heard country music pouring from the open front window. And a man's voice from inside, shouting to someone in another room, "How can you burn spaghetti?" Followed by a woman's laughter.

Eddie pushed the front door open and led the way inside. There was no front hallway. We stood in a small, cluttered living room. A fat brown armchair had a stack of magazines on a square table beside it. A matching brown couch faced a flat-screen TV, a soccer match on the screen.

The mantel over the narrow fireplace was lined with family snapshots.

Eddie's stepfather had a phone to his ear and was pacing back and forth in front of the fireplace. He nodded hello, but kept talking. He was a tall, nice-looking man with a head of thick salt-and-pepper hair brushed straight back, tanned cheeks, and round blue-gray eyes. He had a black-and-white Shadyside Police T-shirt pulled down over ragged denim cutoff shorts.

"My hearing is a month away," he said into the phone. "Can you believe what they're doing to me? Another month I've got to live like this?" He kept gesturing with his free hand, as if the person on the other end was here in the room.

Shaking his head, Eddie guided me into the kitchen. It was bright with white cabinets and a long white counter. Eddie's mom turned from the stove where she was boiling a big pot of spaghetti. "Emmy? Nice to meet you," she said with a warm smile, waving her wooden spoon.

She was really young looking. She had Eddie's wavy dark hair and gray eyes. She was short and very thin, in dark straight-leg jeans and a red-and-white-striped top. "Monday is spaghetti night," she said. "Hope you like pasta. I make a very spicy tomato sauce."

"Love it," I said.

Lou's voice boomed in the other room. I could hear the floorboards creaking under his heavy footsteps.

"Lou is ranting again," Mrs. Kovacs said, turning back

to the boiling pot. "He's talking to his brother up in Buffalo. But his brother can't help him. He's a pharmacist. He can only tsk-tsk."

"Lou just likes to rant," Eddie said, smiling.

"Actually, that's not true," his mom said seriously. "He . . . he's so upset, he can't stop himself." Her voice caught. "And I think he has a right to be upset. I mean, they haven't treated him well. Not at all. And he's been on the force for over ten years."

I turned as Lou came bursting into the kitchen, his face red, waving his phone in front of him. "Tony didn't know what to say," he told Mrs. Kovacs.

She stirred the pot without turning around. "Your brother means well, but he never knows what to say."

"He told me to be patient!" Lou exclaimed. "Do you believe that? *Be patient?* If I wanted advice like that, I'd open a fortune cookie."

His eyes went wide, as if he didn't realize I was there. "Sorry, Emmy," he said. He reached out and shook my hand. He had a huge hand, and I don't think he meant to squeeze my hand so hard. I mean, he practically crushed it.

"Eddie told me about your . . . uh . . . trouble," I said. *Awkward.*

Lou opened a cabinet, pulled out a box of Ritz Crackers, and began tossing them into his mouth. "Yeah. Trouble," he muttered bitterly.

"Go ahead. Spoil your appetite," Mrs. Kovacs said without turning around.

"When is the last time I spoiled my appetite?" Lou shot back. "Like never?"

"We have pasta every Monday," Eddie chimed in. "And Lou makes the meatballs. They're awesome. It's the only thing he knows how to make."

"It's an old Polish recipe," Lou said with a mouthful of crackers. "My grandmother taught it to me. You'd laugh if I told you the secret ingredient."

"What's the secret ingredient?" I said.

"Salt and pepper."

I laughed. Eddie laughed, too. I think he was trying to lift the mood. Maybe get his stepfather to stop ranting and being angry for a few minutes.

Lou studied me. "Your family Polish, too?"

I shook my head. "No. My great-grandparents came from the Czech Republic. I think it was called Czechoslo-vakia back then. I still have some family there. My Great Aunt Marta lives in Prague."

I suddenly pictured the black wolf with the blue eyes. I guess it was because I mentioned Aunt Marta. I felt a tremor of fright, but I forced the image of the wolf from my mind.

Lou shoved the box of crackers back in the cabinet. He turned to Eddie. "No offense. I don't want to embarrass you in front of your friend here. But you'd better take a shower before dinner. You stink, fella."

"I know—" Eddie said, blushing.

"What were you doing? Rubbing dead dogs on your clothes? Rolling around on top of them?"

"Yes," Eddie said. "That's what I was doing, Lou. That's what I do when no one is looking."

"You're funny," Lou said, frowning. He shook his head, his eyes on me. "Not much to laugh about around here, Emmy. The whole town thinks I'm some kind of crazed maniac. One mistake and . . . and . . ."

"Lou, let's try to have a pleasant dinner," Mrs. Kovacs said, finally turning around to face him. "I know you're in pain, dear. But—"

"The funny thing is . . ." Lou said, ignoring her. "The funny thing is, they really need me right now. They're getting nowhere with the robbery investigation. I mean *nowhere*."

Eddie's eyes went wide. I felt my heart skip a beat. We were both suddenly alert.

"Robbery?" Eddie said. "What robbery?"

17.

guess you young people wouldn't want to read a newspaper," Lou said sarcastically. "Where do you get your news, anyway? From *SpongeBob SquarePants*?"

Eddie rolled his eyes. "We don't watch cartoons, Lou. That's more *your* style."

Lou opened his mouth to answer, but thought better of it.

"I have a breaking news app on my phone," I offered.

Lou squinted at me. "And you still don't know about the robbery here in town a few nights ago?"

"Cut her some slack," Eddie said. "Just tell us about it. Come on, Lou. Just tell us what you're so fired up about."

Lou leaned back against the kitchen counter. His big hands squeezed the counter edges, then relaxed, then squeezed again. I could see how tense he was, how he was nearly bursting from his anger.

"It was an armored truck robbery," he said. "At the Division Street Mall. This guy in a ski mask showed up just as they were loading the truck with the money from ten stores for the whole week."

My heart was skipping beats now. I tried to swallow but my mouth was suddenly as dry as cotton.

This is the robbery. This is where the money came from.

"Just one guy with a gun," Lou said. "That's all it took. He didn't even have a buddy, someone to drive. He flashed a revolver and told the truck guys to fill his briefcase with money."

"Wow," Eddie said. "Did he get a ton of money?" Eddie had his eyes on me. We both had the same thoughts. And we both knew we had to force ourselves to act completely innocent and normal.

"Yeah. Thousands," Lou said. He clenched his fists. "Thousands. He tied up the two truck guards, and he got away quickly and cleanly. No muss. No fuss."

I let out a long breath of air. "Unbelievable," I muttered. I couldn't get the image of the brown leather briefcase out of my mind.

"But the robber didn't know one thing," Lou continued. "He wasn't as smart as he thought he was." He motioned us to follow him. "Come here. I'll show you this."

"It's almost time to eat, Lou," Mrs. Kovacs said.

He didn't answer her. He led us to an alcove at the back of the living room. A wooden counter against the wall served as a desk. The little space was filled with bookshelves and files and papers in total disarray.

Lou sat down in front of a laptop and tapped some keys. "Look," he said, motioning Eddie and me closer until we huddled right behind him.

"The masked robber didn't realize he was standing under a security camera," Lou said. "Look at this picture of him. It's grainy, but you can see him pretty clear."

I leaned over Lou's shoulder to get a better view of the laptop screen. I could smell Lou's aftershave, very strong and minty. On the screen, the black-and-white picture was dark. But I could see a guy in a ski mask, holding a revolver. He was big, tall and broad. He wore a dark sweatshirt, very baggy, but you could still see that he had a belly that hung over the front of his dark pants.

"Do you believe it? The guy took a selfie without knowing it," Lou said. "Check him out. He's a big dude. This photo will definitely help identify him when he's caught." He spun around. He stared at Eddie, then turned to me. "Hey, what's your problem?" he demanded. "What's up with you two? How come you suddenly look so pale? I didn't frighten you—did I?"

I don't know how Eddie and I made it through dinner.

I definitely had no appetite after seeing a photo of the guy whose money we stole. My stomach was actually doing flip-flops, and I felt as if my heart had leaped into my throat.

I could see Eddie was totally tense, too. He kept

chattering about school and about his job, telling stories about Mac Stanton, and talking about Danny and Riley. Talking a mile-a-minute. Anything that came into his mind. It wasn't like him at all, but his mom and stepdad didn't seem to notice.

Mrs. Kovacs barely said a word. She kept asking us how we liked the spaghetti. It was actually pretty good, but I had to force myself to eat it. I really didn't feel like eating.

Lou jumped up a couple of times to answer phone calls. He went into the kitchen to talk, but we could hear every word of his conversations since he was shouting and ranting angrily.

Finally, Eddie made an excuse. He said we had to work on a history project at my house. And we made our escape.

"Whew." He wiped sweat off his forehead as we walked down the block to my car. I noticed a tomato sauce stain on the front of his T-shirt. My stomach was still gurgling. I took a few deep breaths.

Eddie put a hand on my shoulder. "Can I drive?"

"You said you don't have a license," I replied. "Remember?"

"I know. I'll be careful. I just feel like driving."

I handed him the key. Actually, I felt too shaky to drive. "Where are we going?"

"Nowhere," he said, sliding behind the wheel. "I just want to drive."

So that's what we did. We drove aimlessly around

Shadyside and eventually found ourselves going up the River Road, the sun dipping low, turning to gold in the river out my window.

"Well . . . that was intense," Eddie said finally. He pulled the car onto the grassy shoulder and put it in park. "Seeing that masked guy . . . it kind of freaked me out."

"Me, too," I murmured. I kept my eyes on the sunset. "So now we know where the briefcase came from."

"And we know who stole the money and hid it in that hollow tree," Eddie finished my thought. He started to slide an arm around my shoulders, but I squirmed out from under it.

"I thought we were talking," I said.

"Of *course* we're talking, Emmy. But what more is there to say?"

"Well . . ." A thought flashed into my mind that sent a shuddering chill down my back. I stared at the setting sun, letting the full horror of my thought wash over me. "That masked guy . . ." I finally found my voice. "He's going to come after his money."

"I know," Eddie said, "but he's not going to find it. And he won't know where to look for it. *No way* he'll know it was us who took it."

Didn't Eddie see that I was suddenly trembling in fear. Couldn't he tell that a cold chill had descended over my entire body?

"Eddie," I said softly. "Eddie, listen to me. He'll know we took it. He'll definitely know."

Eddie narrowed his eyes at me. "Huh? How will he know?"

"Eddie, you carved our names on the tree. You *gave* him our names. It won't take him long. He'll figure out who we are, and he'll be coming. He'll be coming real soon."

PART
THREE

18.

Eddie finally caught on. Something flashed in his strange gray eyes, and his face suddenly went rigid. He reached for me, and I sank into his arms. We sat there holding each other, not speaking, not moving, our faces pressed together. No sound but our breathing and the soft lap of the river current below us.

We held each other until the sun vanished and darkness swallowed the car. Headlights washed over the window. An oncoming car honked at us. The sound snapped us out of our terrified paralysis.

I sat back up. I could still feel Eddie's warm cheek on my skin. I gazed out the window, searching for the moon, but I couldn't find it. "If only . . ." I whispered.

"If only *what*?" Eddie said, his hands sliding over the steering wheel.

"If only we had left that briefcase in the tree," I said. "We'd be safe, Eddie. Sure, we wouldn't have all that money. But we'd be safe. That guy will be desperate. And he has a gun. He'll kill us, Eddie. When he finds us, he'll *kill* us."

I tried to hold it back, but a sob escaped my throat. And my body shuddered once again. I wrapped my arms around my chest, trying to stop the shakes.

"Okay," Eddie said, locking his eyes on mine. "Okay. He won't kill us, Emmy. That's what we'll do. That's exactly what we'll do."

I gazed back at him. "What are you saying?"

"We'll return the money. We'll dig it up and put it back in the tree."

Another car whirred past, filling the windshield with white light.

"When?" I said. "Right now?"

Eddie shrugged. "Why not?"

My mind was spinning. "What about the others?"

"We'll tell them later. We'll tell them what we did. They'll understand. They're our friends, right?"

I nodded. "And their lives aren't in danger. Not like us. They'll understand we had no choice."

Eddie started the car. A sharp wind gust came off the river. The air was surprisingly cold. I rolled up my window.

I suddenly felt lighter. The idea of giving back the money made me feel so relieved. I couldn't wait to get back to a normal life.

Eddie was whistling to himself, tapping a rhythm on the steering wheel. I could see he felt better, too. He turned the car around, and we roared down the River Road toward the pet cemetery on the other end of town.

Strong wind gusts battered the little car. Gazing out the window, I saw that the sky had turned an eerie yellow. "Is it supposed to rain?" I asked.

Eddie nodded. "Yeah. Looks like a pretty good storm coming up. Let's try to beat it." He tromped hard on the gas pedal and the car shot forward.

"Hey, wait—" I grabbed his sleeve. "No way. Remember? No license?"

He slowed a little. We passed the mall. A line of cars was leaving. The stores were closing. I thought of the armored truck parked there, probably near the Shadyside First National Bank, although Eddie's stepdad didn't say. I pictured it parked there, its back door open. And the masked gunman holding out his briefcase to be filled.

Eddie was obviously thinking about it, too. "That guy must be pretty bold to hold up an armored truck all by himself," he said.

"Or pretty crazy," I added.

Eddie nodded. "Know what? I'll bet it was an inside job. Probably a guy who worked for the armored car company."

I squinted at him. "Why do you say that?"

"Because . . . how did he know when they'd be loading the truck?"

"He'd probably been at the mall watching for weeks," I said. "You know. Getting the schedule down."

"Maybe. But someone would have noticed him," Eddie said. "Lou said the guy showed up at just the right time. When they were piling the money for the whole week into the truck." Eddie shook his head. "The guy had to have inside knowledge. That wasn't just luck. I'll bet one of the armored truck drivers was in on it."

I groaned. "What's up with you? We're not detectives. We don't care who did it or how or anything. Let the police worry about that, okay? Let's just make sure we never have to run into the guy."

"Okay, okay, Emmy. You've got to chill. We're both way tense, okay. I was just talking. You know. Nervous talking. I don't care who the guy is, either. But let's keep it together. We'll dig up the money, take it to the Fear Street Woods, and stuff it back in that tree."

We rode on in silence. A few raindrops spattered the windshield. The wind swirled around the car. I crossed my fingers and prayed the storm would hold off till we returned the briefcase and were out of the woods.

Eddie pulled the car up to the pet cemetery. The gate was locked, but he knew a gap in the fence that we could slip through. I shivered as we found a path through rows of graves. There were raindrops carried on the wind, but so far, no downpour.

"We should have brought a flashlight," Eddie said. "The storm clouds are so low, the sky is pitch black."

"We didn't know we were coming here, remember?" I

said. My eyes were slowly adjusting to the darkness. I could make out the low gravestones on both sides of the path.

What was that howling sound? A wolf?

No. Just the wind through the trees.

Stop it, Emmy.

I spotted a shovel resting against a fat tree trunk in back of a grave. I grabbed it and handed it to Eddie. "You're in business," I said. "Now we just have to find the right grave."

"Not a problem," he said, his words muffled by the wind. It blew his hair straight up, as if his hair was reacting in fright. Any other time, I would have laughed. He looked so stupid. But it was too creepy here to laugh. I reached out my hand and smoothed his hair down for him.

He turned and led the way down the dirt path. I could see the outline of Mac's office and living quarters on the other side of the cemetery. The windows on the little building were all dark.

Darkness everywhere.

Eddie stopped at the end of the row. We stepped over a clump of tall grass. The grass was wet and I could feel the cold water seep into the legs of my jeans.

The grave in front of us looked newly dug. The dirt was still in clumps, not smooth. "This is it," Eddie murmured.

And as he said those words, the wind suddenly stopped. As if somebody had turned a switch. We stood there staring at each other in the sudden silence. Such a deep hush. As if the whole planet had stopped. As if we had died and were covered by the silence of the grave.

Stop it, Emmy.

Every muscle in my body was tense. My teeth hurt because I was clenching my jaw so tightly. I gazed around. Nothing moved. Nothing.

"Maybe the storm will miss us," Eddie said, breaking the silence, his voice strangely hollow on the still air. He dug the shovel into the lumpy layer of dirt and began to dig. The blade sliced easily through the loosely packed dirt, and in a few minutes, Eddie had dug up a low mound at the graveside.

"Almost there," he said, mopping his forehead with the back of his hand. His hair was damp and matted to his head. "I only buried it three feet down."

"Hurry," I said. "I . . . I can't stand the smell here. Why does it always smell so bad? Is it the dead animals?"

Eddie shook his head. "I don't think so. They're all in coffins. And buried deep. It's got to be coming from somewhere else."

He lowered his head and shoulders and dug the blade into the soft dirt.

After a few more minutes that seemed like *hours* to me, he stopped and leaned on the shovel handle. He peered down into the hole he had dug. "This is definitely where I buried it," he said, talking to himself, not to me. "On this side of the grave. I remember it clearly. This is how deep I dug."

He sighed and mopped his forehead again. "Oh, well." He jumped into the hole and began digging with the shovel in again. Tossing the dirt up frantically now, muttering to himself, groaning with each heave of dirt.

I leaned toward him. "Eddie? Sure this is the right grave?"

"Of *course* I'm sure! I'm not stupid! This is Sparky's grave. I dug it myself," he shouted angrily. "Shut up, Emmy. Just shut up."

Startled by his anger, I took a few steps back.

He heaved the shovel away. It bounced off the next gravestone and landed at my feet.

Then he dropped to his knees in the grave and, groaning loudly with each move, began pawing at the dirt, scrabbling it up with both hands. Clawing big clods of dirt up like a frantic animal, spitting and cursing, tossing handfuls over his head. Finally, he cried out a string of curses and raised himself, chest heaving, to his feet.

"It's . . . gone," he gasped, eyes wide, sweat pouring down his face. "Someone took it. The briefcase is gone."

19.

I reached out and helped tug Eddie up from the hole. His hands were caked with mud. Even in the dim light, his dark hair glistened with sweat. His whole body trembled as I pulled him up and held him, wrapped my arms around him, waiting for his panting breaths to slow.

Finally, he heaved a long sigh and shook his head hard, as if shaking away his anger and surprise. I stepped back, and he wiped his mud-caked hands on the legs of his jeans. Then he swept back his hair, which had fallen down over his forehead.

"I don't know what to say," I stammered. "One of our friends? One of our friends came back and took the money? I really can't believe that, Eddie. I really don't think—"

"It had to be Danny," he said, his voice hoarse. He picked up the shovel and slammed it with all his might onto the ground. "Of course it was Danny."

"No," I said. "That's crazy. Why do you think—"

Eddie started stomping toward the car, an angry scowl

on his sweat-drenched face. "He was the only one," he said. "The only one who wanted to take his share without waiting."

"But that doesn't mean he came back and took it," I said, hurrying to catch up with him. "You need to calm down, Eddie. We need to figure this out. But you have to get yourself together."

He wheeled around, his eyes wide with anger. "I'll get myself together—as soon as I get the money back from Danny." He pulled open the car door and dropped behind the wheel.

I hesitated. I'd never seen him this crazed before. I didn't like it. I was frightened, too. The armored truck robber was going to come after Eddie and me to get his money. And we didn't have it.

But going insane and blaming our friends wasn't going to help us.

"Are you coming or not?" Eddie called.

"Hey, it's *my* car," I said. He started it up before I was in my seat. "Where are we going? Don't tell me we're going to Danny's."

"Of course we're going to Danny's," he murmured, pulling the car away from the cemetery fence.

"But we don't have any proof—" I started.

"Proof? Emmy, why do we need proof? I'm just going to ask him nicely to return the money. He'll act real innocent. You know Danny's a good actor. He's in the drama club. He's in all the plays. Danny likes to act. So . . . he'll act all innocent. And then I'll persuade him to tell us the truth."

"I don't like this, Eddie," I said. "Seriously. You're out of control. What do you mean you'll *persuade* Danny?"

He didn't answer. He tromped his foot on the gas and we sped through a stop sign.

"You and Danny are best friends," I said, trying to get through to Eddie, trying to make him see he wasn't thinking clearly. "How long have you been best friends? Why are you so convinced your best friend would do something to hurt you?"

Eddie snickered. "Ever look up the word *naïve*?"

"Huh? What are you saying? I'm naïve because I would never accuse my best friend of stealing?"

"It's not about friendship," Eddie said, squealing the car around the corner onto Park Drive. "It's about money. That's all it's about. And Danny needs money. You know he didn't get the scholarship to Loyola. So his plans are totally screwed up."

I started to reply, but I didn't know what to say. I knew that Danny was hot-headed and liked to get his way. But he was a good guy. Even though he broke up with me last winter, I still had feelings for him. He was still a friend.

I thought about how he reacted that night when Eddie and I told him about the money we found. Danny really did seem desperate, eager to take his share right away.

But was he desperate enough to betray his friends?

Eddie and I didn't talk the rest of the way. I watched his

eyes follow the yellow cones of our headlights, his jaw clenched tightly. His hands squeezed the steering wheel as if he was trying to strangle it.

"Eddie, please—" No. I gave up. I could see there was no reasoning with him.

Eddie bounced the car to a stop in Danny's driveway, nearly bumping the back of the SUV parked in front of the garage. He swung his door open and jumped out. Then he raced to the front stoop without looking back or waiting for me.

I hurried to catch up to him. He rang the doorbell. I heard chimes inside the house. The porch light flashed on and, a few seconds later, Danny's father opened the door.

Mr. Franklin is a short, trim man, very young-looking. He could pass for a twenty-year-old, I think, except there are patches of gray in his red-brown hair. He squinted at us through his black-framed glasses. He wore baggy blue shorts and a sleeveless T-shirt that showed off his skinny, pale arms.

"Hey, guys," he said. "It's kind of late." He had a bottle of Miller Lite in one hand. "You looking for Danny?"

"Who is it, Shawn?" I heard Mrs. Franklin call from inside.

"Danny's friends," he called back to her. He opened the screen door and gestured with the beer bottle for us to come in.

"Sorry. We lost track of the time," I said.

"Danny's up in his room," Mr. Franklin said. "He has

battle fatigue from playing *World of Warcraft* for two hours instead of doing his homework."

"I'll do my homework in homeroom." Danny said, appearing behind his father. He eyed us both. "What's up?" He gazed at Eddie's mud-caked jeans. "You have an accident or something?"

Eddie didn't answer. His jaw was still clenched tight. "Can we talk?"

"How are your parents, Emmy?" Danny's mom called. "I saw your mom having lunch at Driscoll's, but I didn't have a chance to say hi."

"They're fine," I said. "Mom is going back to work at the junior college in the fall."

"Nice. Tell her I said hello."

While this conversation was going on, Eddie and Danny had a staring match. Mr. Franklin took a long drag on his beer bottle, then disappeared into the living room.

"Let's go out back," Danny said. "You two look grim. Everything okay?"

"Not really," Eddie answered.

We followed him out the kitchen door to his backyard. They have a patio out there with a picnic table, a charcoal grill, a hammock, and several comfortable wicker chairs. Danny started to sit down, but stopped when he saw that Eddie and I intended to stand.

"So? What's up?" Danny said, scratching a side of his face.

"Just give us back the money, and there won't be any trouble," Eddie said.

Talk about getting right to the point.

Danny jerked backward as if he's been slapped. He narrowed his eyes in confusion and glanced from Eddie to me. "What did you just say?"

Eddie squeezed his hands against the waist of his jeans. "I said give back the money."

Danny's eyes went wide. He seemed unable to process Eddie's words. "You mean the money we buried? It's missing?"

"I told Emmy you'd play dumb," Eddie raised his hands and balled them into tight fists. I took a step back. I tensed every muscle. If Eddie started a fight, I knew I'd have to try to break it up.

I'd learned a lot about Eddie's temper tonight, and I wasn't very happy about it.

"But . . . I *am* innocent," Danny protested, his voice rising. "You think I took it? Are you serious?"

Eddie nodded, his gray eyes cold as ice.

Danny let out a bleating sound, like an injured goat. "I don't believe you," he told Eddie. "I don't believe you are accusing me. Aren't we friends? I thought so. We all agreed that night in the woods. We agreed to leave it buried till it was safe. So why would you accuse me? Why do you think I would break our agreement?"

Danny's fists were knotted, too. The two boys were breathing hard now, standing stiffly, their backs arched, like cats preparing to attack.

"Because you wanted the money. You really wanted it,"

Eddie said, his eyes locked on Danny's, as if trying to penetrate into his brain.

"We *all* wanted the money," Danny said. "All of us. And guess what, Eddie? Most of us didn't trust you. We didn't trust you to keep it safe for us. And now you're here telling me the money is gone. Very convenient. Do you really think you can fool us by accusing me?"

Eddie lunged at Danny. Danny stumbled back against the picnic table.

I uttered a cry. "Stop!"

Before Danny could stand up, someone jumped out of the bushes at the side of the house. Someone big and heavy came charging out of the deep shadows. And when his face came into the light, I could see it was twisted in anger.

"Riley?" I called. "What are *you* doing here?"

20.

Riley let out a cry, lowered his head, and tackled Eddie around his waist. Eddie dropped to the patio stones with a hard *thud*. Riley landed heavily on top of him.

Danny and I both stared down at them as they wrestled, grunting and groaning at our feet. My mind whirred: *What is Riley's problem? Has he gone crazy?*

Finally, Riley gave Eddie a hard shove that made Eddie grab his gut. Riley rolled away from him and climbed heavily to his feet. His nose was bleeding. He rubbed it with the sleeve of his T-shirt.

Danny squinted at Riley. "Didn't your mother teach you any manners? First you say hello. Then you beat the crap out of someone."

"You never were funny," Riley muttered, mopping at his nose. He turned to Eddie, who was still on his back on the patio floor. "Where's the money?"

Eddie groaned, holding his stomach. "I think you broke a rib or something."

"Where's the money?" Riley screamed. "The money is gone, Eddie. And you took it."

Danny had his eyes on the back door. "Shut up, Riley. My parents are in the living room. They'll hear you and be out here in a second."

Riley scowled at Danny. "The money is gone." He wheeled around to face Eddie, who had slowly climbed to his feet. Eddie stood unsteadily, squinting at Riley as if he didn't understand what language he was speaking.

"We all trusted you," Riley said, letting the blood flow from his nose over his lips and chin. "You promised you'd keep it safe. But I knew you'd take it."

Eddie swallowed a few times. "You went to the grave? You dug it up?"

Riley nodded. "I didn't trust you. I went to check, and I was right. You pig, Eddie. I knew you'd take it."

Eddie raised both hands. "Wait. Wait. When, Riley? When did you go to the grave?"

"After dinner. About seven. Why?"

"Eddie and I went to the grave to check on the money," I chimed in. "We were there after ten, I guess. And the money was gone."

"I *know* it was gone!" Riley boomed. "Don't try to lie for him, Emmy. I know who took it! I know who the *thief* is!"

"No, Riley—*please!*" I screamed as Riley came at Eddie again.

He pulled back his huge fist and pounded it hard into

Eddie's belly. And as Eddie started to collapse, Riley smashed him hard under the jaw.

Eddie uttered a weak groan, shut his eyes, and crumpled to the ground, folded in on himself.

I stared in horror. "Eddie? Eddie?"

He didn't move.

21.

I think you should go to the emergency room," I said. I was down on my knees beside Eddie, who was sitting up, working his jaw with one hand.

"It isn't broken," he said. "I'm okay, I think."

"The doctors should check you out," I said. "You know how they always talk about internal bleeding on TV shows."

"I'm okay. Just sore," he said. I tried to help him stand up, but he waved me back. He climbed to his feet, still working his jaw. "See? No problem. Just drive me home. I'll be fine."

Riley had vanished after knocking Eddie out. He ran back into the shadows at the side of the house and disappeared the way he had arrived. When Eddie opened his eyes and sat up, Danny went inside the house. He didn't want his parents to become suspicious.

"Are you sure you can walk?" I said, holding Eddie's arm.

He nodded. "Yeah. I can walk. Do you believe Riley? Was he out of his mind or what?"

"I think all three of you were acting crazy, Eddie. You were ready to fight Danny."

"But I didn't attack him like a madman," Eddie said, rubbing his jaw. "Riley didn't give me a chance."

"Did you and Riley fight before?" I asked. "Did you have issues with him?"

"Not really. We weren't good friends or anything. You know. We just found ourselves in each other's classes and sometimes we hung out." He let out a long breath. "But that big hulk is nuts. He is seriously psycho."

I held Eddie's arm and led the way to the car. He was walking unsteadily. And I saw that his jaw was starting to swell.

He groaned as he lowered himself into the passenger seat. He gazed up at me, holding his gut. "Is it possible to break a stomach?"

"Probably just sore," I said. "I can take you to the ER. Really."

He pulled the car door shut. I climbed behind the wheel, feeling shaky, my heart doing butterfly flips in my chest. I started to slide the key into the ignition, but he grabbed my wrist. "Let's just sit and talk for a few minutes."

"Okay." I settled back against the seat. I stared out at the purple night sky. No stars. The porch light went off on the front of Danny's house. The light in the front window flashed off, too.

"So . . . the briefcase was gone hours before you and I went to dig it up," Eddie said. "It was already gone by the time Riley showed up there at seven."

I nodded. "I don't think Danny took it. Did you see the shock on his face? That wasn't acting."

"Then, who?" Eddie said. His voice sounded strained, I guess, because of his swollen jaw. "Was it one of our friends? Or was it someone else?"

I turned to him. "You mean—?"

"Was someone else watching us that night? The night we buried the money there? Could someone have seen us and come back later for the briefcase?"

"I had a strange feeling that night," I said. "That we were being watched. But it was just a feeling. I didn't see any-one."

Eddie gazed out the window in silence for a long time, thinking hard. The houses on Danny's block were all dark now. It was nearly midnight. I knew I'd have to sneak into the house. I hoped I could get into bed without waking Sophie.

Eddie leaned forward suddenly, his eyes wide. "I just thought of something." He grabbed my arm. "The security cameras."

I squinted at him. "The what?"

"Mac installed those security cameras, remember? Because so many people were dumping dead dogs in the cemetery at night. Maybe one of the cameras—"

"Will show us who stole the briefcase." I finished his

sentence for him. "Yes! Maybe one of the cameras was aimed in the right direction, and we can see who it was."

Eddie's silvery eyes locked on mine. "I think we can check the recordings tomorrow after school. Mac said he was going to be away for a day or two."

"It's a date," I said. I started the car and headed for Eddie's house.

Sophie sat up in bed the moment I stepped through our bedroom door. "Emmy? What's up?" She rubbed her eyes. Her short black hair was matted to one side of her head. She brushed a hand through it.

I sighed. I'd hoped she wouldn't be awake. "Did I wake you up?"

She shook her head. "I wasn't really asleep. I was waiting for you."

I kicked off my sneakers and quickly changed into the silky blue nightshirt I'd left draped over my dresser that morning. Then I dropped onto the edge of my bed, suddenly feeling a heavy wave of weariness roll over my body. I yawned, my eyelids heavy.

Sophie appeared wide awake now. "So where were you?"

"With Eddie," I said.

"No. Really," she insisted. "You never stay out past midnight on a school night. Where were you?"

"Not your problem, *Mom,*" I said nastily.

Her head pulled back. I could see she was hurt. "Emmy,

I'm your sister. You can't tell me anything? Am I like an enemy or something?"

I could feel the weariness pressing me down. And then another feeling. A feeling like I had to tell someone what was going on. A sudden strong urge to confide in Sophie. Not just because it would make me feel better to share the story with someone. But because it might help change Sophie's harsh attitude.

Sure, I had a guilty conscience. I felt terrible about Sophie's resentment of me and her feeling that I didn't care about her and didn't want her to be close to me. But somehow, I never did anything to make anything better.

Now, feeling so exhausted and so frightened, so totally unsure of what I should do, I decided to tell Sophie everything. I crossed the room to her bed, dropped down beside her, and began to talk, my eyes on the floor, my voice just above a whisper.

I started to tell the story, and it just poured out of me. I told her again about the overnight campout in the Fear Street Woods. Yes, for some reason, I wanted to start at the very beginning.

Then I told her what I kept from her the first time. I told her about finding the briefcase in the hollow tree, about how it was filled with thousands of dollars.

"Oh, wow. Oh, wow." Sophie kept shaking her head. "You're not making this up?"

"It's all true," I said. "It sounds crazy. I know it doesn't sound real, but—"

"Emmy, what did you do with the money?" she demanded. "You didn't take it—did you?"

"Yes," I replied in a whisper. "We all decided. It . . . it was so much money, Sophie. It would change our lives forever. We took it."

Her face filled with confusion. "But . . . what did you do with it?"

I told her everything. How we buried it in the pet cemetery. How I was afraid the robber was coming after us because Eddie carved our names on the tree. How someone dug up the briefcase and the money was gone.

"I- I'm so frightened," I stammered. "It was so exciting at first, Sophie. So thrilling to think about how we could spend thousands of dollars. But now . . . it's a total nightmare, a dangerous, frightening nightmare."

I took a deep breath. My heart was pounding. The words had just spilled out of me, and now I felt more exhausted than relieved. Looking up, I glimpsed tears in Sophie's eyes.

She leaned across the bed and wrapped me in a hug. "Emmy . . . you're shivering," she whispered, holding me tight.

We stayed like that for a long moment, our cheeks pressed together. When we pulled apart, I felt a little embarrassed. Sophie and I weren't the huggy type. We almost never touched each other.

"Thank you for telling me about it," she said softly, wiping her eyes. "Thank you for trusting me."

I didn't know how to respond to that. I just lowered my gaze and sighed.

"Is there anything I can do to help?" Sophie asked. "Anything at all?"

I raised my eyes to her. "I don't think so. But . . . I'm glad we can talk like this."

I crossed the room to my bed and climbed under the covers. A warm breeze fluttered the curtains at the open window. Sophie clicked off the light.

So weary . . . so exhausted. But my mind was still spinning. Surprisingly, I fell asleep quickly. Fell into a deep sleep and found myself in another dream that seemed as real as my waking life, the colors so vibrant, my vision so clear. I could smell the fresh air. Something sweet on the air.

In the dream, I was running, running on all fours through the sweet-smelling pasture. Tall grass brushed my sides. I thudded heavily, pounding out a steady rhythm.

I'm an animal, I told myself in the dream. I lowered my fur-covered head and trotted, the grass nearly up to my face, tickling me, brushing me with its prickly blades.

Day became night, and I was running through darkness. Running under a full moon, quivering above me.

The dream ended suddenly at the edge of the pasture.

I woke up in the darkness of my room. Saw the fluttering window curtain. And raised my head to howl.

Sitting up in bed, I howled like a wolf. Howled at the window, my wails shrill as a siren, howled and couldn't stop.

And then Sophie was beside me. She wrapped her arms around my body as I howled. "It's okay," she said calmly, quietly. "It's okay. It's okay." She repeated the words until I lowered my head and became silent.

"It's okay, Emmy," Sophie said. "I won't tell Mom and Dad. I promise. I won't tell them what's happening to you."

22.

promise. I won't tell them what's happening to you."

I thought about Sophie's words all day in school. I couldn't think about much else.

What IS happening to me?

The answers were too frightening. Too weird. Was I going totally insane?

I was desperate for a distraction. I tried to shut everything from my mind as I drove to my after-school job.

Three days a week, I have an after-school job as a nanny. I take care of this sweet little boy named Martin in a house four doors down from Shadyside High. Martin is only fourteen months, and he's just learned to walk and to run. This means he falls down about a hundred times an hour.

It's fun to take care of him. He babbles nonsense words all the time I'm there. But the hard part of my job is keeping right beside him and making sure when he falls a hundred times that he doesn't hit his head or get a bruise that might cost me my job.

I know that sounds cold. Of course, I worry about Martin, too. But his mom pays me really well, and I'm desperate to keep this job.

His mom got home from her job around five thirty, and Martin went wobbling over to her, his arms raised high in a nice greeting. I gave her a short report on all the games we had played and what Martin had eaten. Then I said, "See you next time," and hurried out the door to my car.

And that's when I noticed the man dressed all in black, large dark shades covering most of his face, watching me from a little gray car parked directly across the street. I stared for a moment, frozen, trying to determine if he really was watching me or if I was imagining it because of my current paranoid state.

He didn't look away.

His window was rolled down. He had one arm resting on the door of the car. Of course I couldn't see his eyes, but his head turned as I stepped up to my car.

He's definitely watching me.

And then my brain made a big leap. *He is the armored truck robber.*

He saw my name on the tree trunk. He figured out who Eddie and I are. He's come for his money.

Each thought sent a stab of fear to my heart.

It was a wild hunch. But I knew I was right.

I pulled open the car door and squeezed behind the wheel. I shut the door and locked it. My hand fumbled the key in the ignition. The key fell from my hand and dropped to the car floor.

I heard the man's car start up across the street. Breathing hard, I swept my hand over the floor, found the key, and stabbed it into the ignition. My car was beeping insistently in my ears, telling me to strap on my seatbelt. But I didn't have time. I had to get away.

I floored the gas pedal, and the car squealed away from the curb. I had to hit the brake hard for a stop sign at the corner. A woman was pushing a stroller across the street, tugging a tall dog on a leash behind her.

I almost hit them. I could have killed them both.

I shouldn't be driving. I'm too frightened to think clearly.

Raising my eyes to the rearview mirror, I saw the little gray car make a U-turn and start rolling toward me. "Come on! Come on!" I shouted at the woman. She dropped the dog leash and struggled to retrieve it. "Come on—move!"

Finally, they stepped onto the sidewalk. I made a sharp right. I saw the gray car close behind. Saw the man's big sunglasses through his windshield. Saw his grim expression.

Another hard right took me onto the street behind the school. I saw a couple of teachers talking in the staff parking lot. One of them shouted at me as I roared through a stop sign.

I spun the wheel hard, careened onto the curb. The wheel bounced in my hands. I twisted it hard to the right.

Regained control. And swung the car onto the road that cuts through Shadyside Park.

"Look out!" I screamed as I nearly hit two girls on bikes. I swerved at the last second. They both cried out. One of them fell over onto the grass. I didn't slow down to see if she was okay.

I roared through the park, the light dancing on the windshield, shadows from the tall trees making the glass light, then dark.

I glanced into the rearview mirror. Was he still there?

Yes. The gray car roared close behind me. Sunlight filled the windshield, making it impossible to see. But I knew he was in there, staring at me in the dark shades, following me because . . . because . . .

He wanted his money.

I shot out of the park without looking for traffic. Squealed into a turn lane. Bombed forward, not breathing, not thinking, so terrified, the car was driving *me*. I had no control. I couldn't think. I couldn't make my muscles move. My teeth were clamped so tightly shut, my jaw ached.

My whole body tight, tensed. I glanced into the mirror again.

Gone. The car was gone.

"Huh?" A sigh escaped my throat. I eased my foot on the gas pedal, my eyes locked on the rearview mirror. Did I lose him? Was he waiting for me in the next block?

The street behind me was clear. I sat there, panting like a dog, my chest heaving up and down, not blinking, just staring into the mirror. Until finally . . . my senses returned. My breathing slowed.

I wiped my cold sweaty hands on my shirt and driving slowly now, slowly and steadily, turned the car toward the pet cemetery. "Eddie," I said out loud. "Eddie, he came after me. He'll come again, Eddie. He'll come again."

The parking lot was empty. I squealed the car to a stop beside the front gate. I couldn't see Eddie in the graveyard. Was he already in Mac's office? He was supposed to wait for me outside.

I pulled open the gate and slipped into the cemetery. The putrid smell greeted me, carried on a hot gust of wind. I held my breath and trotted along the dirt path between the two rows of low graves. My legs felt rubbery and my heart was still thrumming in my chest after that terrifying car chase.

I spotted Eddie at the side of Mac's building. He had his back against the wall and was texting rapidly on his phone. "Eddie! Hey—Eddie!" I shouted his name, my voice high and shrill. I stumbled over an upraised tree root, regained my balance, and ran up to him.

"A man followed me, Eddie. He followed me in his car. He was wearing a hoodie and his face covered with these big, dark shades."

Eddie tucked the phone into his jeans pocket. His eyes went wide. "You think . . . ?"

"Think it was the robber? Yes. Of course," I said. "He

waited for me outside the Robertsons' house. I started to drive here and he came after me." I grabbed Eddie's sleeve. "What are we going to do?"

"Find the money," Eddie said. "He knows we took it. If he gets to us, and we don't have it, he'll . . . kill us."

I gave Eddie a shove. "You're not doing a very good job of cheering me up."

He shrugged. He pulled open the office door and motioned for me to enter. "Know what will cheer me up?" he said. "Finding whoever stole the briefcase from the grave. Getting that money back."

The front office was surprisingly clean and tidy. A desk, a file cabinet, a bookshelf, files and papers neatly stacked. The walls were covered with framed photos of dogs and cats, dozens of them. Probably portraits of the pets who were brought to be buried or cremated.

"The security monitor is in back," Eddie said. I followed him through a narrow door that led to a small backroom. This room was cluttered and dark with cartons stacked at one wall, shovels leaning at their side, folding chairs stacked nearly to the ceiling, an empty case of water bottles.

"Over here." Eddie stood at a counter against the fall wall. A small video screen flickered in front of him beside a stack of electronic equipment. "We can rewind this and see if there's a camera aimed at the right grave," he said. "Pull over two of those chairs. This might take a while."

I dragged two chairs over and we sat in front of the monitor. I could see a fuzzy black-and-white image of the front of the graveyard. Eddie fiddled with the controls, and the picture began to wriggle as the recording rewound.

"Riley was here last night at seven," Eddie said, eyes on the screen. "So the money must have been stolen the night before." He leaned over the video player. "Hey, there's a timer. I can go right to that night."

He pressed some keys. The picture flickered, then remained solid. "Hey—that's it," I said. "Isn't that the grave where we buried the money?"

Eddie studied it, leaning close to the monitor. "Yes. We're lucky. The camera is in the right place."

We both sat on the edge of our chairs, gazing at the black-and-white image. I could see the flat rectangle of dirt and beyond it, dark trees. Nothing moved. It was like staring at a photograph.

I clasped my hands tightly in front of me. I stared so hard, the image became a total blur. "Nothing happening," I said quietly. "No one there, Eddie."

He raised a finger to his lips. "Just keep watching." He didn't take his eyes off the screen. He leaned over the control box and fast-forwarded it slowly.

He stopped when something moved.

A shadow at first. The shadow covered the screen for a moment. Then the black faded to gray, and I could see it was a person. "Eddie, look!" I whispered.

Eddie nodded, eyes on the screen.

The figure moved quickly to the edge of the grave. He was big, very wide, and he wore a black hoodie. The hoodie was pulled up to hide his face.

"Who is it?" I whispered. "Do you recognize him?"

Eddie shook his head.

We watched the silent image. The big hooded guy had a shovel. He glanced in both directions, then started to dig. His head was down. Hidden under the hood, there was no way to see his face.

He dug quickly, steadily, tossing the dirt to the side of the grave. I could see he was very strong. He had no trouble plunging the shovel blade deep, then heaving the dirt aside.

"I don't believe this," Eddie muttered, shaking his head. "Who is it? Come on—lift up your face so we can see you."

We watched the big guy toss the shovel aside. He bent into the hole he had dug and pulled up the briefcase. He brushed it off with one hand.

And as he turned to take the briefcase away, his hood fell back—and his face was revealed.

Eddie and I both uttered cries of surprise as we stared at the face—so clear . . . so clear—on the little screen.

It was Riley.

23.

Eddie backed up the recording and we watched it again. The big guy pulled up the briefcase, brushed it off, and turned away from the grave. And as he turned, his hood fell back. And we could see clearly that it was Riley.

He set the briefcase down carefully. Then he picked up the shovel and began to fill in the hole he had dug. When he finished, he turned and walked casually away, the briefcase tucked under one arm.

Eddie and I watched in total silence, too shocked to speak. Finally, Eddie jumped to his feet, shaking his head, his eyes wide with confusion. "I don't believe it. Riley accused me. He beat the crap out of me. He . . . he seemed so angry."

"He put on a good show," I said. "He wanted to make sure we didn't suspect him."

"So he pounds me unconscious just to throw us off the track?" A bitter scowl crossed Eddie's face. "Great friend." His hands were shaking as he fiddled with the camera equipment and returned it to live recording. "Let's get out of here."

I followed him to the front office. We shut off the lights. Outside, the sky had clouded over. I could see dark trees against the pink-gray clouds.

Eddie took long strides toward the car with his fists tight at his sides.

"What are you thinking?" I asked, hurrying to stay up with him.

"Payback time," he said, eyes straight ahead.

I stepped in front and stopped him. "You're not going to fight him, Eddie. That's just dumb."

"I have to get that money back."

"Let's all get together and confront him," I pleaded, blocking his path. "A meeting. We'll get Danny and Roxie and Callie. We'll tell them what we saw. Then we'll all go face Riley. We're all in this together, Eddie."

He nodded. "Okay."

I hoped he meant it.

Riley wasn't in school the next day. Someone said he had the flu or something. I wondered if that was true.

The rest of us couldn't get it together to set up a meeting about him. It's kind of impossible to get five people organized by text messages. Eddie said he couldn't wait. We had to confront Riley before he did something with the money. Eddie said it had to be tonight.

After school, I went to Sophie's track meet in the stadium behind the school. It was part of my new *Be Nicer to Sophie* campaign. The Shadyside High team was competing against a team from Dover Falls, a few towns down the highway. A few parents had traveled from Dover Falls to see the event. And there were scattered Shadyside kids and parents in the stands. But the stadium was about 90 percent empty.

So I was happy to be there to support my sister. She waved to me with a smile as she trotted out for her first competition. Sophie ran in two events, a 100-meter sprint and a 400-meter sprint. I found myself shouting and cheering as she ran.

She finished second in both events. I thought she might be disappointed, but she seemed really happy as we walked home after the meet. "I don't care about finishing second," she said, practically skipping as we crossed Park Drive. "Those were my best times ever in both events."

"Awesome," I said. I tried to sound enthusiastic, but I suddenly found myself thinking about Riley, and the blurred image of him on that security monitor flashed back into my mind.

Sophie kept chattering about how she needs these new track shoes and how she was working on her body angle to be more aerodynamic and how she was sure the shoes would help her trim even more time off her 400-metre speed.

I'll tell you one thing about running. It definitely pumps you up. I never heard her talk nonstop like that.

And then Mom greeted us at the door with some interesting news. "Hey, girls, I received a letter today," she started.

Sophie rolled her eyes. "Thanks for asking how my track meet went."

Mom's cheeks turned pink. "Oh, sorry, dear. I've had my mind on so many things, I—"

"I had my best times ever," Sophie said. "Too bad you couldn't be there like some parents." She refused to cut Mom some slack.

"She was impressive," I chimed in. "Like a rocket."

"Nice," Mom said. "I'll be at the next one. I promise."

Sophie rolled her eyes again. "For sure," she muttered.

"Anyway, I'm trying to tell you about this letter," Mom said, leading the way into the kitchen. She picked up a long white envelope off the counter. "It's from your Great Aunt Marta in Prague."

"Is she okay?" I asked.

Mom nodded. "Yes. She's fine. In fact, she's coming to visit."

My mouth dropped open. "Really? She's going to fly here? But isn't she about a hundred and twenty?"

Mom chuckled. "At least," she said, running the envelope through her fingers. "Yes, she's very old but I guess she's strong enough to travel. She says she wants to see you girls one more time."

"Wow," Sophie said. "That's amazing."

"It makes me nervous," Mom confessed. "She's so old . . .

and so strange. She has so many weird ideas. You know. Superstitions. Stuff from the Old Country."

"Is she your aunt or Dad's aunt?" I asked.

Mom thought about it for a long moment. Then she shrugged. "We both always called her Aunt Marta. I think she was just a really close friend of my grandparents. Not related at all."

"I don't remember her much," Sophie said. "Is she seriously weird?"

"You'll see," Mom said. "She's different. But you'll like her. She has a million interesting stories."

After dinner, Sophie and I were up in our room. I was struggling with some trig problems. Yes, I'm math phobic but I don't see the point in talking about it. Sophie was staring at her laptop screen, watching a video of her track meet from the afternoon.

When my phone buzzed, I grabbed it up, happy to be interrupted. I glanced at the screen. Eddie. "Hi, what's up?"

"Danny and I are doing it," he said.

"Huh? Doing what?" I could hear that he was in a car.

"Going to confront Riley," he answered. Danny said something but I couldn't make out what it was.

"Eddie? You're going to Riley's house?"

"Yeah. We're going to get the briefcase back."

My brain was spinning. Did they have a plan? Did they think they could fight Riley? What were they going to say to him?

"Wait for me," I said. "I'm coming. Can you hear me? I'll meet you at Riley's house. Wait for me, okay?"

What could I do? Maybe stop them from acting like total jerks? Maybe stop a fight before it starts? I didn't know if I could help or not, but I wanted to be there.

I shut my trig notebook and started to pull on my sneakers.

Sophie raised her head from the laptop. "You're going to Riley's house? Does he have the briefcase?"

"Eddie and Danny are going there to get it back from him," I told her. "I'm a little scared. They might get him angry. Riley is so big. He doesn't know his own strength."

Sophie jumped to her feet. "I'm coming with you. I can't let you go by yourself."

I sighed. "Okay. Come with me." My throat suddenly felt dry as cotton. I tossed her the car keys. "I realized I was too tense and frightened to drive. Do you mind driving?"

"Not a problem," Sophie said, squeezing the keys in her fist. She stopped at the mirror to straighten her short hair and adjust the collar of her pale green top. I knew my hair was a mess, but I didn't care. I just wanted to get to Riley's house and stop Eddie and Danny from doing anything crazy.

Sophie adjusted the driver's seat and the mirrors. She's two years younger than me, but she's two inches taller than I am. She backed down the driveway, and aimed the car toward Riley's house.

A light rain pattered down, raindrops glowing on the

windshield in the lights from an oncoming car. I pressed my head against the headrest. I could feel the tension tightening the back of my neck.

Suddenly, I started to feel strange. Woozy. The bright light flashing in the windshield lingered in my eyes. I tried to blink it away, but I could see only a wall of white.

What is happening? What is happening to my eyes?

I realized I was just frightened, filled with heavy dread. The slice and scrape of the windshield wipers repeated in my ears, echoed, grew louder. The light flickered, faded and became blindingly bright. The wipers ticked in my ears. I shut my eyes tight against the flickering light.

I'm passing out. I'm going to faint.

I feel so weird.

What is happening to me?

24.

When I opened my eyes, Sophie and I were standing in someone's front yard.

How did this happen? Did I totally blank out?

Didn't Sophie realize there was something wrong with me?

I forced the questions away, struggling to make sense of everything. It took a few seconds for my eyes to focus. I'd been here before. I squinted into the wash of moonlight over the front of the square white house. The dark shingles appeared to glow at the sides of the wide front window. A bike leaned against the wall of the front stoop.

Riley's house. Yes. As it all came into focus, I realized I was standing in Riley's front yard.

Sophie huddled close beside me. She had the car keys tight in her fist. She had her other hand on my shoulder. "Are you okay, Emmy? You looked weird in the car. I was going to pull over, but—"

"Where is Eddie?" I asked, still struggling to shake away

the fog in my brain. "Did we beat Eddie and Danny over here?"

Sophie shrugged. "I don't know. I'm as confused as you are."

I took a deep breath. "Should we go knock on the door?"

Sophie nodded.

I took a few steps—then stopped. My eyes locked on the low hedge that ran along the front of the house. What was that draped over the hedge? Hanging so awkwardly over the hedge top . . . arms spread . . . legs folded . . .

Oh. Oh. Oh no. I opened my mouth in a shrill scream of horror.

Face down over the hedge. Riley.

Riley on his stomach, his legs spread at a weird angle, arms hanging out at his sides. Face down. Riley face down. Face buried under his hair, buried in the hedge branches.

I staggered forward for a step or two. Sophie clung to my side. Another step. And then I screamed again.

Riley's clothes had been ripped away. His skin ripped away.

He's been clawed to pieces!

I clapped my hands over my face. I didn't want to look, but I couldn't pry my eyes away.

His bare shoulders had long claw lines over them, all caked with gleaming red blood. His shirt was in strips. The skin on his arms had been clawed raw and red.

I gasped as I pictured raw meat. A huge hunk of raw meat. One of those hunks of beef they hang on those big hooks in meat lockers. And the dark stain over the hedge. . . . the dark stain was Riley's blood.

Unable to keep my balance, I lurched forward—and glimpsed his face, half-hidden under his hair. A pulpy mass, like hamburger meat.

Sophie grabbed me around the waist and tried to tug me away. "Don't look!" she cried. "Emmy—don't look!"

Too late. Too late.

I couldn't stop gaping at the maimed and butchered body. I couldn't take my eyes away from the most horrifying sight I'd ever seen in my life.

25.

At Riley's funeral three days later, I stared at the closed coffin. And I pictured the shredded body inside, mangled and torn, glistening red meat and strips of skin.

I couldn't stop picturing it. It stayed in the front of my mind, the first thing I saw when I woke up. The last thing I saw when I closed my eyes at night.

I heard the sobs and sighs at the funeral. I didn't hear the minister's words, and I didn't hear the words Riley's brother spoke. I didn't hear the hymns his family had chosen. I heard the crying and I pictured Riley's body sprawled over the hedge, and I thought about the past few days. And the police officers and their questions . . . hours of questions. And the bits of frightening news that came to us a piece at a time.

Did the police have a clue as to how Riley was murdered?

They had a theory.

The front lawn had been soft from an early rain. And in the soft dirt, the police had found animal tracks.

Wolf tracks. In the dirt all around the low hedge and along the front of the stoop.

And so the police concluded that Riley had been attacked by a wild animal. Their guess: It had been the same wolf that had attacked a dog in Shadyside Park.

No human could have caused the body this kind of damage, they said. The tracks and the trail of blood on the lawn gave the police a few clues. Riley had been attacked as he stepped off his front stoop. He had struggled with the wolf, but he was no match for it. The creature attacked Riley, clawed him until he stopped moving, then left him draped over the hedge.

The wolf had to be rabid, a veterinarian said on the news. Wolves don't attack humans, even when provoked. The wolf must be sick, crazed.

The police called Sophie and me to the station and questioned us with our mom across the table. We were the only ones there that night. His parents were at the movies. Eddie and Danny hadn't arrived yet.

We tried to tell them everything we knew. But how could we be helpful? We really didn't know anything. We hadn't seen a wolf—or anything—in the front yard or in the neighborhood.

Of course, there was a lot we didn't tell the police. The briefcase of money was never mentioned. But it didn't have anything to do with Riley's death—did it?

Roxie was silent during the whole funeral. She kept to herself at the back of the church. She came to my house after the funeral, along with Danny and Callie and Eddie. Eddie kept his arm around my shoulders as we shared the armchair across from the couch.

Roxie stayed by herself in the corner by the fireplace, as far from us as she could get. She kept her arms tightly around her chest. Tears ran down her cheeks in jagged rivulets. And her expression of anger and disdain remained on her face that entire afternoon.

Danny was serious and quiet, which was a change. He tapped his fingers tensely on the arm of the couch. Callie clung to him, her green eyes misted by tears, her normally perfect blonde bangs matted and disheveled.

Roxie kept her eyes down. She muttered something none of us could hear.

"We know how terrible you must feel," I said. "We're all devastated, Roxie. I think we're all in shock. I can't eat. I can't sleep. I haven't been able to think of anything else since that—"

"Bet you can think about the money!" Roxie snapped, jumping to her feet. "Liars. You're all liars. You're not thinking about Riley. You're thinking about the briefcase and the money. I—I—" She raised her fists above her head. "I can't stand any of you! I hate you! Liars!"

She uttered a curse and stomped out of my living room. A few seconds later, the front door slammed behind her.

The four of us sat in silence for a long moment. The

sound of the door slam rang in my ears. I shut my eyes and pictured Riley's clawed body.

Callie squeezed Danny's hand. She whispered something, and he nodded. Danny raised his eyes to Eddie. "You know what's weird?"

"What?"

"The police searched Riley's house, right? They probably went through every room, looking for clues I don't know, looking for whatever? You know. Like cops always do."

"Yeah. Probably," Eddie said. "What's your point?"

"Well . . . why didn't they find the briefcase? If they searched Riley's house, how come they didn't uncover the money?"

Eddie nodded his head, thinking about it.

"Maybe they found the money and decided to keep it," I said.

Danny snickered. "You mean like crooked cops on TV?"

"Yeah. Maybe," I said.

Eddie was still thinking about it. He turned to Danny. "You think maybe Riley didn't keep the money at home? Maybe he hid it somewhere else?"

Danny nodded. "That's what I'm thinking."

"But where would we start to look?" Eddie said. "We can't exactly ask his parents if they saw him give a briefcase to someone."

Callie uttered a sob. "The poor guy. What a terrible way

to die. I think we should forget about the briefcase and try to go on with our lives." She turned away. I saw tears running down her cheeks.

"We can't just forget about it," Eddie said. "The guy who stole the money . . . he'll be coming for it. If we don't have it . . . he'll . . . he'll . . ." Eddie's voice broke.

A hush fell over the room.

Callie pulled Danny to his feet. "Let's go. We need to take a drive or something. I . . . I don't want to talk about this anymore."

"But . . . all that money," Danny said. "Are we really just going to forget about it?"

"Yes," I said. "We have no choice."

"Shut up! Everyone just shut UP!" Callie screamed, covering her ears with her hands. "I *said* I don't want to talk about it." She went running to the front door. Danny glanced at Eddie and me and then chased after her.

The front door slammed again. Eddie and I were left alone. We held each other, squeezed together on the armchair. We didn't say a word. I don't know what he was thinking. As I pressed my cheek against his, I was trying not to think at all. But, of course, it was impossible.

The doorbell chime made us both jump. *Who could that be?*

We jumped to our feet. Pushing back my hair, I trotted to the front door and pulled it open. "Roxie?" I couldn't hide my surprise.

Her expression was grim. Her face was paler than

before, as white as cake flour, and her chin was trembling. She pushed past me into the living room.

"Here," she said. She raised the briefcase in both hands and pushed it at me. Eddie stepped up beside me, eyes wide with shock.

"Take it," Roxie insisted. "Take it. Go ahead." She shoved it hard into my chest. I staggered back a few steps, wrapping my arms around it.

"I don't want it," Roxie said, scowling at Eddie and me. "I don't want any part of it." Her chin trembled harder. Tears filled her eyes. "Riley gave it to me to hide. But I don't want it. I . . . don't want anything to do with it. Or you."

"But, Roxie—" I started.

She was breathing hard, her chest heaving up and down. "Riley . . . he . . . he . . . the poor guy. He only wanted to protect the money for the rest of us. That's all he wanted. He . . . he wasn't trying to steal it. He—"

She couldn't finish. Her whole body shuddered and she began to sob.

I handed the briefcase to Eddie and stuck out my arms to hug her. But Roxie spun away from me. Still sobbing, she stumbled to the door and disappeared outside.

Eddie and I stared at the front door. I turned to him. He held the briefcase awkwardly by the bottom, pressing it to his chest. I gazed at it until it became unreal . . . a dark brown blur.

He opened it and peeked inside. "It's in there. It's all in there."

I took a deep breath. "Okay, Eddie. What do we do with it now?"

26.

With all the horror, I completely forgot that Aunt Marta was arriving. Two days after Riley's funeral, Mom picked her up at the airport.

She had cherry red cheeks, and dark circles around both eyes, but her eyes were bright and alert and shiny. She wore her straight white hair pulled back in a bun, held together by a wide red ribbon.

She was tiny. Like a miniature person. Like an old doll. When I stepped up to hug her, I had to lean down, nearly bending myself in half. She probably weighed eighty pounds at most.

She didn't wear "old lady" clothes. She wore a colorful flower-print skirt, pleated all around and down to her ankles, and a bright yellow peasant blouse many sizes too big for her narrow frame. A silver cross dangled down from a chain around her neck.

Her "traveling clothes," she said. She told us her six daughters sewed everything before her flight to Shadyside.

"Six daughters!" Mom exclaimed. "I didn't realize . . ."

"Seven would be bad luck," Marta said in her dry whisper of a voice. "Seven daughters in a house is too tempting for the Evil Ones."

Mom, Sophie, and I didn't know what to say to that.

"Six daughters and a son could lead to sunshine and good fortune," Marta continued, gesturing with one bony hand. "But I didn't want to take the chance." She winked a wrinkled eyelid at me. "I'm a practical woman. But I know better than to tempt the fates." She giggled, as if she had made a joke.

Sophie and I carried her suitcase and travel bag up to the guest room. "Why is Mom so awkward around Aunt Marta?" Sophie whispered.

I shrugged. "Beats me. Maybe because Marta is so old and weird?"

Sophie grinned. "Weird? What's weird about bringing sticks from some kind of enchanted forest to hide under her bed? Everyone does that—right?"

"Sshhh. She'll hear you," I whispered.

"She doesn't have any accent," Sophie said.

"You want her to talk like someone in a horror movie? I vant your blood. . . ." I whispered and walked toward her like the Frankenstein monster."

Sophie and I laughed so hard, we couldn't stop. When we finally calmed down, Sophie said: "I've never seen Mom so tense. Did you see the look on her face when she spilled a little of Marta's tea from her cup? And Marta had to chant some kind of tea prayer over it and stir her teaspoon twelve times?"

I laughed. "Marta's weird but she's kind of sweet. She smells like cinnamon. Did you notice?"

Sophie nodded. "Her teeth are so white. Do you think they're real?"

"Yuck. I don't want to think about that," I said. I hoisted Marta's suitcase onto her bed. Sophie pulled the enchanted sticks or whatever they were from the travel bag and slid them under the bed.

Then we went back downstairs to join Mom and Aunt Marta for lunch. Marta sat in a chair at the head of our kitchen table. She was so short, her feet didn't touch the floor.

Mom had her phone to her ear. She lowered it and turned to us. "That was your dad. He'll be home from Atlanta tomorrow." She turned to Marta. "Jason is so sorry he wasn't here to greet you, Marta"

"He was always a day late," Marta said, frowning. "That boy. I remember. Always a day late. I always said he'd be a day late to his funeral."

Sophie and I exchanged glances across the table. Marta seemed serious and a little scary We didn't know whether to laugh or not.

Mom served a tossed salad and tuna sandwiches for lunch. Aunt Marta ate hungrily, taking little chipmunk bites, her red cheeks moving as she chewed.

"Emmy? Do you remember your visit to me when you were little?" she asked. But she directed the question to Sophie not me.

"*I'm* Emmy," I said. "Sophie was too little to remember much of our visit, but I remember a lot."

Marta nodded, taking another sandwich half. She sighed. "This is some age we live in. You jump in an airplane and it takes you to a different world."

"I think you're very brave for making the trip," Mom said.

Marta squinted at her. "Brave?"

"I mean . . . at your age. I mean . . ."

Awkward.

Marta turned back to me. "My village is still part of the Old Country, the world I grew up in. Very different. Very different. In the Old Country the real and the magical live side by side. The old ways and the new ways . . . we have them both."

Sophie lifted her phone off the table. "Do you have these, Aunt Marta?"

Marta nodded her head. "Yes. But it's not the only way we communicate. We communicate in ways you would probably think are not possible."

Very mysterious.

The lunch continued like that. Marta was eager to tell us of the superstitions and traditions of her village. I was surprised that she didn't ask Sophie and me more questions.

She had traveled all this way, but she didn't seem very interested in learning about us.

I guessed that maybe she was nervous, too, about being in a new place. And that she would relax and be more natural as the days went by.

After lunch, she went up to her room to unpack and take an afternoon nap. Mom seemed really relieved. "I'll be so glad when Dad gets home tomorrow," she said.

I studied her. "Mom, why are you so tense?"

She stared back at me, thinking hard. "I really don't know."

I helped her with the lunch dishes. Then I went to my room where Sophie was already doing homework, and I sprawled on my bed and started texting some friends.

That night, I had another wolf dream.

In this dream, I was chasing two white wolves through the woods. Was I a wolf, too? I couldn't see myself. I felt as if I was running on all fours. I could hear the slap of my paws on the leafy dirt floor. And I could smell the tangy fragrance of the deep woods. Even in the dream, I could smell the fragrance of the air, and it made the dream so much more real, so real I wanted to escape it.

But I also knew that was impossible. I had to see where the dream led.

I chased the two wolves through the dark passages between the tall trees. I could hear them panting, steady huffing as they trotted side by side, bobbing their furry white heads.

And then suddenly, they spun around. They rose up on their hind legs, eyes wild, jaws opening, baring their jagged teeth.

Before I could turn away, they attacked. Leaped at me with their forepaws raised, snarling their sudden rage.

I screamed.

And woke up.

And found Great Aunt Marta sitting beside my bed. She leaned forward and brought her face close to mine. "So you have the dreams," she said in a hoarse whisper. "I knew you would."

27.

shook myself awake. The fragrance of the night air in my dream lingered in my nose. I felt half in the woods, half in my bed. I tried to blink it all away.

Marta started to stand up, but I gripped her wrist and pulled her back down to my bedside. "What do you mean?" I demanded. "Aunt Marta, you have to explain."

She stared at me with her dark eyes, gleaming in the light from my bedroom window. I had the feeling those eyes could see right into my brain. See my thoughts. See my dreams.

She gripped the silver moon pendant on my neck in her tiny hand. "The crescent moon," she said. "I gave that to you. Do you wish on the moon, child? Has it granted any of your desires?"

"Huh? No. I mean . . . no."

She set the pendant back on my skin and rubbed it three times. "I gave you the crescent moon because I knew you were the special one."

"But, tell me about the dreams. Why did you say you knew I would have them?"

She didn't answer. But I knew this was my only chance. My chance to learn the truth about me and why I've been plagued with these crazy wolf dreams.

I gripped her wrist again. "Marta," I said, my voice still choked with sleep. "Marta, tell me. Please. Do I have these dreams because of the dog? The dog that bit me in your village when I was five?"

To my surprise, Marta gasped. Her eyes went wide. "Dog?" she said. "Is that what your mother told you? That you were bitten by a dog?"

I nodded. "Yes. She said a dog ran out of the woods and bit me. And I've been having these dreams. . . ."

I glanced over at Sophie's bed. She was sleeping on her side, eyes closed. Was she really sleeping through this conversation? Or was she pretending to be asleep and eavesdropping on us?

"Your mother never wanted you to know the truth, Emmy," Marta said, leaning close, her hot breath brushing my face. "She was afraid, Emmy. So she told you a lie."

I swallowed. My throat was suddenly so dry. "A lie?"

Marta's eyes flashed. "You were bitten by a *wolf*, Emmy."

"Huh?" I gasped. "Not a dog?"

"And it wasn't an ordinary wolf," Marta said, lowering her voice to a whisper, leaning even closer so that her cheek was nearly touching mine. "It was an *immortal*," she said. "It was—"

"Wait a minute," I said, grabbing her bonelike wrist again. "Wait a minute. What are you saying?"

"Listen to me. I've traveled very far so that you will know the truth. The wolf that bit you was an immortal. A wolf creature most people no longer believe in. But it exists. It exists to all of us who live in the Old Country and know the truth of the world old and new."

I stared at her, stared at her glowing eyes so deep in their sockets, so dark, unblinking eyes. "Marta . . . you mean a *werewolf*?" The words spilled from my mouth. They didn't seem real. I didn't even know I was saying them.

Marta nodded. "There are many names." She slid her hand over mine. Her hand was hard and warm. Mine felt wet and cold. "I don't blame you for being shocked, dear. You've never been told the truth. But don't blame your mother."

"I . . . I don't understand," I murmured. "What does this mean?"

Marta shut her eyes. "You are wolfen, Emmy. Listen to my words. You are wolfen."

I stared at her face in the shadowy light. I couldn't breathe. I couldn't move. Her words repeated and repeated in my mind.

And in that instant—the most horrifying moment of my life—I realized that *I killed Riley.*

28.

*A*fter a few silent seconds, Aunt Marta left me sitting up in my bed, paralyzed by my horrifying thoughts. I heard the floorboards in the hall creak as she made her way up the stairs to the guest room. I heard her door close. I heard the wind rush against my bedroom window. I heard the fridge hum in the kitchen downstairs. I heard Sophie's soft breathing. I heard my heart thumping in my chest.

It was as if every cell in my body had gone on alert. My brain was frozen in the horror of my thoughts, but my whole body throbbed as if an electric current was shooting through me.

I'm an animal. I killed someone. I killed Riley.

Will I kill again?

I can't control my dreams. Is there any way to control what I do in real life?

The questions were too frightening to think about alone.

I pictured Riley's shredded body. The glistening red

meat underneath the skin that had been shredded in strips like bacon.

I did that. I became an animal and I clawed Riley to pieces.

Suddenly, I was on my feet. I lurched across the room. I grabbed Sophie by the shoulders and shook her. I didn't mean to be so violent but I was out of my mind.

"Sophie! Sophie!" I screamed her name so loud my throat ached.

Sophie awoke with a startled cry. I felt her back muscles tighten. She whipped around, raised her head, gaped at me with her mouth hanging open. "Emmy? What's wrong? You scared me to death."

"Sorry. Oh. Oh no. Sorry," I said. I took a stumbling step back. "Sophie, you have to listen to me. We have to talk."

"Huh? It's the middle of the night, isn't it?" She squinted at the clock on her bedside table.

"You have to talk to me!" I cried, my voice high and trembling. I dove to the bedroom door and pushed it shut. I made sure it clicked. "Sophie, please—" I said. "I really need you now."

Those words got through to her. Rubbing her eyes, she sat up. She kicked the bedsheet away and stood. "Can we turn on the light? Do we have to talk in the dark?"

"Leave it off," I said. "I really don't want to see anything. I want this to be a dark dream, just a dream, and I want to wake up from it and find that everything is normal, and I am normal, and the world is a happy, normal place, and—"

Sophie grabbed me by the shoulders. "Emmy, stop. You're talking like a crazy person." Her eyes burned into mine. "Tell me. What is it? What is making you act so weird?"

"M-my dreams, Sophie," I stammered. "All those dreams. And my weird feelings. I knew . . . I knew somehow I was different . . . but . . . but . . ."

"Emmy? What's wrong? What are you trying to say?"

I shook my head. "This is too frightening. It's so hard. . . ."

Sophie kept her gaze on me, waiting for me to continue.

I took a deep, shuddering breath. "Marta just told me that I'm a wolf creature," I choked out. "A wolf creature, Sophie. Do you believe that? Marta said it's because of the bite I got."

"You mean when we were kids visiting her village?"

I nodded. "Yes. She said I was bitten by a wolf . . . not by a dog. So I'm wolfen. Because of the wolf bite. Don't you see what that means?"

Sophie blinked a few times. Her face was twisted in confusion. "No. I—I'm having trouble with this, Emmy. It's too much . . . Too hard to understand. What are you trying to say? What does it mean?"

I took another deep breath. "It means I am the one, the one who ripped Riley apart." Those are the words that I was about to say.

But I couldn't bring myself to say them. I didn't want to believe them. And somehow, I guess I thought, if I didn't say it to anyone, maybe it wouldn't be true.

Sophie squeezed my shoulder tenderly. "Emmy? You don't believe Marta, do you? She's a crazy old lady filled with fairy tales and old stories. She—"

"I-I think what she said might be true," I stammered.

Sophie shook her head. "You're my sister. You're not a wolf creature. How can you even think it?"

She was trying to calm me down, trying to make me feel better. But in my heart, I knew Marta was right. Marta was telling the truth. I knew it. I knew it. I knew it.

"Sophie," I whispered, my skin tingling from the cold sweat that covered my body, "you were there with me in Riley's front yard. We haven't wanted to talk about it. But you were there with me. Please help me. What did you see? Did you see Riley's killer?"

Sophie hesitated. She shifted her weight on the bed. "I wasn't there, Emmy. Don't you remember?"

"You weren't there?"

She shook her head. "Don't you remember? I dropped you off. You said you didn't want me there. So I dropped you off at the bottom of Riley's driveway."

I squinted at her. My mind was spinning. I didn't remember any of this. I had blanked out or gone into a trance or something.

"Y-you left me there?" I stammered. "And where did you go?"

"I started to drive home," Sophie said. She shrugged. "I didn't know what to do. I was totally confused. First, you told me to come with you. Then you said you didn't want me. I . . . I was halfway home and then I turned around."

She straightened the front of her nightshirt. "I decided I couldn't leave you there. I knew there could be trouble. I knew that Danny and Eddie were going to confront Riley."

"So you came back?" I asked. I was struggling to make sense of this, struggling to remember any detail of it. But I couldn't.

"I drove back," Sophie said. "And when I pulled up to Riley's house, I saw the flashing red-and-blue lights in the driveway. The Shadyside police. They were already there."

She sighed. "I ran up the driveway. Riley was dead, and one of the cops was heaving up his guts at the side of the house, and everyone was going crazy, and it was horrible." Her whole body shuddered.

"Yes. Horrible," I murmured. You don't know how horrible, Sophie. You don't know that your sister is the animal that killed Riley.

And that I can't help myself. I may kill again.

"I . . . saw you just standing there, staring at Riley's body on the hedge," Sophie said. "I could see you were in shock. I knew I had to take care of you."

"I see," I murmured, my mind spinning.

"I forced you to walk away," Sophie continued. "I had to pull you away. It's like your brain had shut down. I . . . I pulled you onto the front stoop. I made you sit down.

The police said they wanted to talk to you. So I waited with you there. You . . . wouldn't talk to me. You wouldn't say a word."

I nodded, swallowing hard. "I don't really remember," I muttered.

"You were the first to find the body," Sophie said. "It had to be a horrible shock."

"Horrible," I repeated.

I couldn't get back to sleep. How could I, with Marta's hoarse voice repeating in my ear. "*You are wolfen. You are wolfen.*" And Sophie's story of how she found me alone with Riley's mangled body. Alone in the front yard in some kind of trance.

How could I ever sleep again?

I heard Sophie's soft breaths across the room. I raised myself and saw that she had the pillow pulled over her head, both arms wrapped around it. Before I realized it, I was on my feet. My bare feet were hot against the cool floorboards.

I stepped into the silver moonlight, washing in through the open window. I was drawn to the moonlight, to the glimmering silver, to its cool beauty. Drawn to its cold light. And without thinking, I was out the window, my bare feet tickled by the dew-wet grass.

And I was running across the backyard, the night wind brushing my face, rustling my hair, fluttering my nightshirt. And then the next yard and the next, my bare feet wet now and covered in grass. I was running toward the moon, hovering so low in the purple night sky, so close . . . so close . . . just overhead, just out of reach.

Not a dream. I knew this was real. The wet grass under my feet . . . the cold night air against my face . . . all real.

I gasped as something bumped my side.

I heard the thump of running footsteps. And felt another bump. And lowering my eyes from the moon, I saw the dog. Tall and scrawny and gray. It bumped up against me again, then took off, running in zigzags in front of me. A wild-eyed, tailless creature, tongue hanging nearly to the ground from its gaping snout.

I turned and ran toward a thick clump of trees—and saw a second dog. Nearly a twin to the first. Nearly furless, so scrawny I could see its ribs, with the same crazy yellow eyes. Head hung low as it ran beside me, but watching me . . . watching me.

The two dogs crisscrossed in front of me as I ran along a twisting path under the trees. Darkness then silvery moonlight. And the dogs stayed with me. And suddenly there were four or five of them. A tall black Lab and a dark-furred giant of a dog. Barking now. They were all yipping and barking with the excitement of our run.

"Go away! Go home! Go home!" My voice came out in shrill shudders of fright. "Bad dogs! Go home!"

My cries made them stop. They turned to face me. Their big eyes glowed darkly under the pale moonlight. Their chests heaved as they panted, all staring at me now.

Why were they there? Why were they following me? Because I was one of them?

Yes. They knew it. They knew my secret. They knew I belonged with them. We were a pack. A pack of wild animals, running through the woods.

They formed a circle, bodies arched tightly, heads lowered, tails stiff behind them. The circle grew tighter as they closed in on me. I heard a growl. Then another. They bared their teeth, eyes glowing brighter as if anticipating their attack.

"No—please . . ." I uttered a sharp cry.

I started to back up. "Please . . . go away . . . go home. . . ."

And then something grabbed my shoulder roughly from behind. I stumbled back. My hands shot into the air, and I let out a scream that shook the trees.

29.

"Sophie . . . Sophie . . ." I gasped, my chest heaving, the words escaping in a choked whisper.

She threw one arm around my shoulders and motioned to the dogs with her other hand. "Shoo! Shoo! Go home! Shoo! Bad dogs! Go home!"

They hesitated, gaping at us open-jawed, panting noisily. Then, to my surprise, they turned, turned away from us, broke the circle, and took off into the trees. Heads lowered, they trotted away. They didn't look back.

"Sophie . . ." I repeated.

"I followed you," she said, her arm still around my trembling shoulders. "I followed you, Emmy. I was so . . . scared."

I shook my head. I wanted to speak. I wanted to thank her. But the words wouldn't come.

"Don't worry, Emmy." She brought her face close to mine. "Don't worry. I'll keep your secret. I promise."

————

I didn't go to school the next morning. I pretended to have a stomach ache. I needed time alone, time to think. But, of course, there was nothing to think about but how frightened I was.

Dad poked his head in my room and asked if I wanted to see Dr. Harvey. I said no. I had a brief moment where I felt like a little girl. I wanted to rush into Dad's arms and tell him everything.

Luckily, that impulse didn't last long. No way he'd believe a crazy story like that. And he wouldn't be taking me to our family doctor. He'd be rushing me to a psychiatrist's office.

Maybe I needed one.

I heard footsteps and the clunk of a suitcase down the stairs, and I remembered that Aunt Marta was leaving. Leaving after only two days. Dad was driving her to the airport.

Still in my pajamas, I rushed out of my room and down the hall and wrapped Marta in a hug. She looked surprised to see me still home. Her eyes locked on mine. "Luck be with you, my dear," she whispered.

Dad carried her bag to the car. I saw him in the driveway, loading it into the trunk.

"Marta," I whispered. "Please. Tell me. Is there a cure?"

She lowered her eyes.

"Please. Is there? Is there a cure?"

She shook her head no and walked out the door.

30.

After stripping Aunt Marta's bedsheets and putting them in the wash, Mom went to a meeting at her college. The house was empty. I stayed in bed. Downstairs, the washer whirred quietly through its cycles, the only sound now.

I sat sideways in bed and leaned my back against the wall. Morning sunlight washed over me from the open bedroom window. I hugged myself tightly. I was sitting in the warm shaft of sunlight, but I felt chilled, chilled to the bone.

"I'm wolfen. A wolf creature. A murderer. Can I ever trust myself to leave this room again?"

I asked the question out loud. I bit my bottom lip. Hard. To punish myself? To snap me out of my terrifying thoughts? I don't know why. I felt the sour, metallic taste of blood on my lips.

Blood. I'm the kind of creature who craves blood.

Maybe I should have gone to school this morning. Maybe I should have risked it. Here alone in my room, I realized

I'd soon go totally insane. I'd be jabbering and talking to myself and chewing my fingernails off and biting my lips raw.

I crossed the room to my laptop and went online. I did a Google search for werewolf. I started at Wikipedia, where else? I learned that another word for werewolf is lycanthrope.

My hands trembled over the keyboard. "I'm a lycanthrope."

My heart started to pound. I scrolled through several articles. They all said the lycanthrope was a figure of folklore. A mythical figure. I knew better. This wasn't cheering me up. I slammed the laptop shut.

My phone rang, startling me. I grabbed it and gazed at the screen. Eddie. Probably worried about me, wondering why I'm not in school. In all my horror, I had forgotten about Eddie. And the briefcase of money. It seemed so unimportant now.

I let it ring. I couldn't talk to Eddie now. I didn't want to see him. I didn't want to see anyone.

I really cared about Eddie. Cared enough about him to worry that I might go out of control again. What if my wolfen powers returned when he was with me? Would I kill Eddie the way I killed Riley, and not remember it at all?

Ohmigod.

All the horror movies Sophie and I had watched together

since we were little . . . Why did I enjoy them so much? Was I drawn to them because I am a creature from a horror movie?

I skipped lunch and took a long nap for most of the afternoon. My sleep was dreamless, as far as I could remember. Sophie had track practice after school, so I had the house to myself till Mom and Dad came home.

Dinner was a blur. I was there at the table with them and I wasn't there with them. I made an excuse for my silence and my lack of appetite. I said I still wasn't feeling like myself. A stomach thing, I told them.

Mom felt my forehead for a fever the way she always does. If you tell Mom you hurt your leg, she'll feel your forehead. It's her only kind of doctoring.

Mom and Dad discussed what a character Aunt Marta is. They laughed about her weird superstitions and Old World ideas. And how she came all this way for only two days. Crazy. I couldn't laugh. I knew the old woman wasn't funny. She had to bring me horrifying news. Not laughs.

I excused myself before everyone was finished. Mom tried to stop me. "I made strawberry shortcake—your favorite."

"Maybe I'll have it for breakfast," I muttered.

I started down the hall to my room when the front doorbell rang. Since I was nearest to the door, I pulled it open. Eddie. His features tight with worry. "How are you feeling? Are you sick? I tried to call."

"I'm kinda sick," I said. I blocked the doorway, a subtle hint for him not to come in. But he didn't pick up on the hint. He pushed past me.

"Feel better? You look okay."

"Thanks for the compliment, Eddie." I didn't mean for that to come out so cold. I just didn't want to see him. I was afraid of how much I'd say. If I told him the truth about me, he'd run. He'd be scared to death. Or, he'd think I'd gone totally nuts.

He grabbed my arm. "I have to talk to you, Emmy. Can we go someplace?"

"Who's here?" Mom called from the kitchen.

"It's Eddie," I shouted. "He brought me my homework."

"Hi, Eddie," Mom called. "Did you have dinner. We have macaroni and ham."

"I already ate, Mrs. Tyler. Thanks." He brought his face close to mine and whispered. "I need your help. We have to talk."

I led the way to my bedroom and closed the door. I knew that Sophie wouldn't barge in. She would probably think Eddie and I were fooling around in here.

I motioned Eddie to my desk chair. I dropped down on the edge of my bed, still all messed up from my long afternoon nap. He glanced tensely around the room. "I didn't know you shared a room with your sister."

"Of course you didn't know," I snapped. "You've never been up here before."

He laughed for some reason. Just from nervousness, I

think. I instantly felt bad for snapping at him. I decided to make an attempt to act more normal.

But I sighed, realizing nothing would ever be normal for me again.

"What's up?" I said. "Did I miss anything in school?"

He shrugged. "Who cares about school? I can't stop thinking about the money in the briefcase, Emmy. I can't think about anything else."

"I don't care about the money anymore." That's what I felt like saying to him. "I'm an animal, Eddie. And I'm a killer. And a hundred bags of hundred-dollars bills isn't going to help my life at all."

But I didn't say any of that. Just gazed across the room at him, waiting for him to continue.

"I hid the briefcase in my room," Eddie said in a low voice. He had his eyes on the bedroom door. "But I don't think it's safe there."

I squinted at him. "You mean you think someone will steal it?"

He shook his head. "No. But my mom is a clean freak. She cleans every room in the house five times a week, including mine. And I think she might find the briefcase. And then Lou will have a million questions for me. And he'll turn the money in. He'll be a hero for turning the money in, and he'll get back on the force. And . . . and we'll be back where we started. Totally broke."

"Maybe that's a good thing," I said, sweeping my hair back over my shoulders. I stood up. I felt so restless, as if my whole body was coiled tight. I started to pace back and forth in front of Eddie. "Maybe it would be good to be done with this whole thing. Maybe give it back to the guy who stole it. Or turn it in to the police."

"No way!" Eddie protested. "I'm obsessed, Emmy. It's all I can think about. I've changed my mind about it. Why not try to keep it? We've worked too hard to lose the money. And it's going to change our lives. All of us."

I stopped pacing. "So what do you want to do? Do you have a plan?"

He nodded. "I want to bury it in the same grave in the pet cemetery."

I uttered a short cry. "Seriously? Are you crazy?"

"No one would ever think of going back there. No one will ever think of looking for it there." He jumped to his feet. "Sure, it sounds crazy. But it's also smart." He grabbed my shoulders. "Come help me, okay? Come with me. I want to do it tonight."

I hesitated. "No, Eddie, I—"

I couldn't think of an excuse. I had a sudden impulse to say, "Look, Eddie, I'm never leaving the house again. I can't explain. But I'm never going out again."

That's how insane my mind was. That's how frightened I felt.

But I saw the intense expression on his face. He needed me. He needed my help. "Okay. Let's go," I blurted out.

"We'll be quick," Eddie said. "I promise. I know you're not feeling well. I'll go into Mac's office and shut off the security camera. Then we'll bury the briefcase, and we'll be out of there. It won't even take half an hour, Emmy. I promise."

"Okay," I said. "I'll make an excuse to my parents, and I'll go with you."

I told them Eddie and I were going to Callie's house. We stepped out into a warm, damp night. It had rained at dinnertime, and the air was still steamy, the lawns glistening under a low half-moon.

We drove to the pet cemetery in near silence. Eddie started to tell me about Lou and how angry he was that his hearing to get back on the police force had been postponed. "It's glum at my house," he said. "I mean, Mom and I tiptoe around the poor guy."

"Too bad," I muttered, only half-listening. I pictured Aunt Marta sitting by my bedside, whispering, "You are wolfen."

"And Lou is berserk. Seriously," Eddie continued. "He threatened to ground me because I left the house with my sneaker shoelaces untied. Believe that?"

I forced a laugh. "Whoa. That's crazy enough."

"He's a lunatic," Eddie said. "He's not acting like himself at all. Mom and I can't wait for him to go back to work and get out of the house."

We had to slow down as we passed the middle school. Cars were streaming out of the parking lot. Some kind of school carnival had just ended. I saw kids walking with their parents, carrying helium balloons and big stuffed animals.

I sighed. I had this strong desire to go back . . . back to being a kid where everything in my life was normal, and my biggest problem was whether or not to get my ears pierced.

I snuggled against Eddie, wrapping a hand tightly around his arm, pressing my cheek against his shoulder. I stared at the passing streetlights until they became a yellow blur. I tried not to think about the briefcase filled with money in the trunk. Would we ever get to share it? Would we ever enjoy it?

Headlights filled the rear window. The car filled with light.

I let go of Eddie and spun around. I couldn't see the car behind us. I could only see the bright white glare of its headlights. The car was right on our tail.

I gasped. The frightening car chase . . . the man who chased after me before . . . coming after me again. In the glare of the headlights through the back window, it all flashed back into my mind.

"Eddie—he's here." I squeezed Eddie's arm. "Behind us. He's the one who followed me—I just know he's the guy who robbed the armored truck. He wants the money!"

Eddie squinted into the rearview mirror. "You sure he's the guy you saw?"

No.

The car swept past us. I saw two women in the front seats. "Oh, wow." I let out a relieved sigh as the car made a sharp left and rolled away.

Eddie turned to me. "Are you okay?"

"I'm not being paranoid," I said. "That man will be coming back for his money."

"He's had plenty of time to find us," Eddie said. "If he's so eager to get his money, where is he?"

I saw the way Eddie was looking at me, studying me. "You think I made up the car chase?" I said, my voice shrill. "You think I made up the man in black? How he came after me through the park?"

Eddie was silent for a long moment. "What if he was just some guy messing with you, Emmy? Or what if you only imagined he was following you?"

"You really think I'm crazy?" I cried.

"You lost him so easily," Eddie said, stopping for a light. "If he was a holdup guy desperate for his money, do you really think he'd let you get away? Don't you think he would drive you off the road or do anything to stop you and force you to talk?"

"I—I—I—" I was too upset to answer. I knew what had happened that afternoon. I knew that guy was coming after me. What was Eddie trying to prove?

"You're just being stupid," I said.

He pulled into the cemetery parking lot. "Sorry," he murmured. "I'm just tense, I guess. I mean, we're both stressed."

"So you believe me about the guy in black?"

He opened the door and climbed out. I didn't hear his answer.

A half-moon hovered over the pet cemetery as I followed him out of the car. Eddie opened the truck and handed the briefcase to me. It felt heavier than I remembered.

"Follow me," Eddie said, glancing up and down the empty parking lot. "You can wait near the grave. Don't get too close till I disable the security camera."

"But won't Mac hear you?" I asked, my voice hollow in the still night air. "You said he lives above the office."

Eddie shook his head. "Mac has a new girlfriend. He's been staying at her place."

I held the briefcase in front of me, both hands on the handle, and followed Eddie to the small rectangular grave. The ground was soft and muddy from the afternoon rain.

"Stay in the darkness here. This will only take a second," Eddie said.

I watched him trot toward the office. I realized I had drops of cold sweat on my forehead. I didn't wipe them away. I gripped the briefcase in both hands.

There was no breeze. Everything was still . . . still as death. The stench in the air was overwhelming. I tried to hold my breath. I stared toward the office, but Eddie had disappeared inside.

The soft *thud* of footsteps behind me made me spin around.

I gasped as the animal came into focus. Moving along the row of graves, it had its head lowered. Its angry eyes glowed like burning coals. The creature was panting loudly, and even in the darkness, I could see the fur raised on its back.

The wolf.

The black wolf from my dreams.

It arched its body, coiled back on its hind legs—and with a ferocious snarl, leaped at me.

A shrill scream tore from deep in my chest. My cries rang off the trees, echoing my horror again and again.

31.

E mmy? Emmy? What is it? What's wrong?"
Eddie was shaking me by the shoulders.

His gray eyes locked on mine. "Why did you scream? What did you see?"

My body shuddered. My mouth hung open. I forced myself to breathe. I spun out of his grip and gazed all around, the sound of my scream lingering in my ears.

"I saw . . . I saw it. . . ." I struggled to form words.

"What did you see?" Eddie gently took my face in his hands. "Did that dog scare you?"

I squinted into the wash of moonlight and saw the tall dog across from us at a row of low graves. A black Lab. It sat on its haunches, ears down, eyes trained on us.

"It . . . startled me," I said.

No way I would tell him that I'd mistaken it for a wolf. That I imagined that the black wolf from my dreams attacked me. No way I wanted Eddie to know how crazy I was becoming.

I took a deep breath and held it. I forced myself to stop trembling.

"Guess I'm a little shaky these days," I murmured. "Ever since Riley . . ."

"We're all shaky," Eddie said. He tugged the sides of my hair. "But we'll be okay."

No, we won't, I thought.

The black Lab climbed to its feet and loped away. Eddie laughed. "Did you think you were seeing a dog ghost?"

"Not exactly," I replied.

"Let's get the money buried and get out of here," he said. "I think we'll both feel better when the money is safe in the ground." He picked up a shovel and started to dig.

I watched as Eddie buried the briefcase. He smoothed the dirt over it carefully so the grave wouldn't look fresh. We drove back in silence.

Sophie was asleep by the time I got home. I was glad. I couldn't handle any more discussions.

The night air remained hot and still. I changed into my lightest nightshirt. I buried my face in the pillow and tried to sleep. But I knew it was hopeless.

I felt wide awake. Totally wired. And my brain was spinning with all kinds of frightening thoughts.

If I fall asleep, maybe I'll dream. Maybe I'll dream about the wolf again. And if I do, maybe I'll transform again.

The hours dragged by. I stayed up all night, watching the moonlight out the open window.

When the alarm buzzed in the morning, I felt as if a truck had run over me. Every part of me ached. My head felt heavy as a bowling ball. It took all my strength to sit up and climb out of bed.

Sophie was already dressed for school. She narrowed her eyes at me. "What's wrong, Emmy? Are you still feeling sick?"

"Just tired," I said. "I couldn't get to sleep."

"Are you going to school today?" she asked.

I hesitated. Then I decided. "Yes. Yes, I am." I couldn't bear another day in my room alone with my thoughts.

I offered to drive Sophie to school, but she said she was meeting a friend from the track team and they would walk to school. I drove slowly, carefully, unable to stop yawning. A whole night without sleep can make you feel seriously weird.

Danny and Callie were the first people I saw when I stepped into the school building. I had a suspicion they'd been waiting for me. It was early, and only a few kids were at their lockers, emptying their backpacks before homeroom.

"How are you?" Callie asked. "You missed the Trig quiz yesterday."

"I'm okay," I lied. "My stomach . . . it just felt weird, but I'm okay today."

Danny glanced around, making sure no one was nearby. "Are we ever going to split up the money?" he asked in a harsh whisper.

I shrugged. "I don't know. Eddie says—"

"I know what Eddie says," Danny said. "But some of us don't agree with Eddie. Some of us think—"

Callie hushed him as two teachers walked by.

"It isn't safe to take it now," I whispered. "The guy who stole it—he came after me. He chased me. He must know that Eddie and I took it."

"That's more reason to take the money now," Danny said. "We can't just hand it back to him."

Callie hung back. She looked pale and scared.

"What do you think?" I asked her.

She shook her head. Her eyes went wide. "I . . . I don't know. I could really use the money. But . . . if you and Eddie are in danger . . ." Her voice trailed off.

I saw Roxie step into the front entrance. She glimpsed us for a second, then walked right past us, eyes straight ahead.

"Hey, Roxie—" Danny called to her. But she kept walking and didn't turn around.

"She doesn't want to know us anymore," he said, watching her till she turned the corner. "I wonder if she still wants her share."

"Danny, what's wrong with you?" Callie slapped his arm. "Is that all you can think about? Just money?"

"Yes," he said. "Just money."

Callie made a disgusted face.

He grabbed her shoulder. "Look, I miss Riley, too. I miss him a lot. I think about him all the time. I'm just saying . . ."

"We know what you're saying," Callie said sharply. She turned to me. "Maybe the four of us should get together?"

I nodded. "Yes. Definitely."

How could I tell them the money wasn't the most important thing on my mind? How could I tell them I really didn't care what happened to the money now?

I am a lycanthrope. I killed Riley. I became an animal and killed Riley.

Why should a lycanthrope care about money?

I realized Callie was staring at me. I wondered if she could see me trembling. For a moment, I thought maybe she could read my terrifying thoughts. But of course that was crazy.

Crazy.

I saw Eddie at fourth-period lunch. We shared a ham-and-cheese sandwich and a bag of tortilla chips his mom had packed for him. I told him about my talk with Danny and Callie.

Eddie shook his head. He crinkled up the brown paper lunch bag. "I had the same conversation with Danny," he said. "I don't know what to tell him. I really think we should wait till . . . till we know we're okay."

I told him I'd drive him to his job at the pet cemetery after school. I tried to change the subject. You know. Think of something cheerful to say. But my head still felt like a rock, and I couldn't think of anything cheerful.

After school, I made a plan with Mrs. Quinn to make

up the Trig quiz. Then I loaded my backpack and made my way out the back door to the student parking lot.

I waved to Sophie in the stadium behind the parking lot. She was warming up, doing stretch exercises with her track team friends. "See you at dinner!" I shouted. I'm not sure she heard me.

I looked for Eddie, but he hadn't come out yet. I turned and strode down the row of cars. I spotted my car at the end near the lot exit. The bright sunlight filled the windshield. I walked around to the driver's side.

I was only a few feet away when I realized someone was sitting behind the wheel. Someone in my car.

"Eddie?" I called to him. But I realized immediately that it wasn't Eddie.

He was too big to be Eddie.

Too big and dressed in black.

In the white sunlight, it took a few seconds to recognize him. I uttered a frightened gasp as he finally came into focus. And I saw the big sunglasses covering the top part of his face.

His straight black hair fell over his forehead. He turned when he saw me approach and pushed open the driver's door.

Too late. Too late to run. I started to spin away. But I was too close, only a few feet from the car.

"Emmy?" His voice was a deep growl. "We have to talk."

32.

My heart racing, I staggered back. He moved quickly. He shoved the car door open—and dove out of the seat, moving so fast . . . so fast for such a big man.

He hurtled over to me and grabbed my arm in his big hands. He was wide and broad-shouldered. He wore a loose-fitting black suit. His shades caught the sunlight. I couldn't see his eyes at all.

But I could see the hard lines on his face. And I could see the threatening scowl that tightened his features.

"L-let me go," I stammered. "Who are you? What do you want? Why were you following me?"

"I think you know what I want," he said. His breath smelled of cigarettes. I saw a bulge under his jacket. He must be carrying a gun.

That thought made a cold shudder run down my body.

He tightened his grip on my arm and brushed the hair off his forehead with a quick snap of his other hand.

"Get off me! Let me go!" I cried. "You're making a mistake. You must have the wrong person. You—"

"You don't want to play games with me, Emmy," he said, speaking in a harsh rasp.

I hated the way he said my name.

And then his eyes were over my shoulder. He was gazing across the parking lot. And I heard a familiar voice. "Emmy? What's up?"

Eddie trotted up to us. His backpack bounced on his back. He stopped, and I saw his eyes go wide. He recognized the man from my description. "You—" he started.

"You must be Eddie," the man said. "You two are the names on the tree, right?"

I didn't see any point in lying. "Right," I said. My legs were trembling. I suddenly felt sick, about to vomit. *He has a gun under his suit jacket. Does he plan to use it?*

He stepped aside and pushed my car door shut. "It's too crowded here," he rasped. "Let's take a walk in the park." He motioned to Shadyside Park, the large wooded park that stretches behind the high school.

Eddie stuck his jaw out. "What if we don't want to go?"

The man snickered. "You're a tough guy? You want to be a tough guy with me? I don't think so." He patted the bulge under his suit jacket. Then he leaned menacingly toward Eddie, sticking his face up close to Eddie's, challenging him.

Eddie lowered his eyes in surrender.

The man took each of us by an arm and guided us past

the parking lot along the stadium fence into the park. I glimpsed my sister again. She was huddled with a group of her teammates.

Turn around, Sophie. Please turn around, I pleaded silently. See this guy leading us away? Get help. Go get help.

But she had her back to me. She didn't turn around.

The park opens up with a wide lawn. Several paths curve into the trees. The man kept his tight grip on our arms and led us to a round wooden band shell. Concerts were given here a hundred years ago, I guess. I've never seen it used for anything except to provide cover when you're caught in the park in the rain.

"Over here," he ordered. We stopped behind the falling-down structure. I glanced back toward the school. No one could see us back here.

He let go of us and brushed his hair out of his eyes again. He had beads of sweat on his broad forehead. He pulled off the sunglasses and rubbed his fingers over the bridge of his nose. His eyes were cold and hard.

"What do you want?" I managed to choke out. I struggled not to shake.

"Let me ask the questions," he said, sliding the shades back into place. "Do you have the money?"

Eddie and I exchanged glances. Was it worth trying to fake him out?

"We don't know what you're talking about," Eddie said.

The man snickered, more of a cough than a laugh. "Yes, you do know," he said quietly.

I wanted to confess, tell the truth. I didn't care about the stolen money. We didn't know how dangerous this guy was. I wanted to tell him where the money was so he'd let us go.

But Eddie seemed determined to play innocent. "I carved our initials on the tree months ago," he told the guy.

"Months ago?" An unpleasant smile crossed the man's face. "It looked fresh to me. I'm not an expert on tree carving, but . . ."

Eddie shrugged. "Why are you asking us about the tree? About money? We don't know anything."

The man shook his head, then spit on the ground, narrowly missing Eddie's sneakers. He studied Eddie for a long, tense moment. "Know what?" he said finally. "It'll go a lot easier on you two if you tell the truth." He patted the gun bulge on the breast of his jacket again. "Know what I mean?"

I couldn't take it anymore.

"Are you going to hurt us?" I blurted out. "Are you going to kill us?"

He turned to me. "I don't want to hurt anyone. But I need to find the money."

Eddie was telling me no with his eyes, but I was too frightened to hold out any longer. This man was dangerous, and he had us trapped. He wasn't going to believe Eddie's innocence act.

"We—we have the money," I said.

Eddie muttered a curse.

"Where?" the man asked softly, his voice low and calm now. "Where is it?"

"We can take you there," I told him. "Right, Eddie?"

Scowling, Eddie agreed.

"If we give it to you, will you let us go?" I asked. If only my legs would stop trembling. My head was throbbing now. I could feel the blood pulsing at my temples.

The man stared at me through the large, round shades. "Let's go," he said. "We'll go in your car." He kept behind us as we made our way back to the student parking lot. "Don't try anything funny. Don't try to signal anyone, hear?"

"You didn't answer my question," I said, my voice cracking. "Are you going to let us go?"

"Just take me to the money."

33.

The drive to the pet cemetery was the longest ride of my life. Eddie drove. The man sat beside him. I hunched in the back, fighting to keep my lunch down, my arms crossed tightly in front of me.

"You found the money in the tree?" the man asked, eyes on the road in front of us.

"Yeah," Eddie said. "We were camping overnight in the woods, and we found it."

"So you took it and you did what with it?"

"We'll show you," Eddie said. "We buried it. In the pet cemetery in Martinsville. To keep it safe."

The man snickered again. "Safe from who?"

"Just safe," Eddie said. "Our friends . . . we didn't want to take it and use it if . . . if it wasn't safe."

"But you planned to keep it? You planned to divvy it up and keep it?"

Eddie hesitated. "Yeah. We did."

We were silent for the rest of the trip.

There were two cars in the cemetery parking lot. I recognized Mac's Jeep at the far end where the tall iron fence ended. Eddie directed the man to the side entrance.

We climbed out of the car. Eddie slid his arm around my shoulders. "It'll be okay," he whispered.

"What makes you think so?" I muttered. I knew he was just trying to help get me through this. But I was too frightened to fool myself. This man could kill us once we gave him the money, and no one would see.

We led the way through the row of pet graves. I had to force my legs to move. My heart beat so hard, I was gasping for breath.

"Which way?" the man demanded. He couldn't hide his impatience. He gazed around. "Weird place. Suckers actually pay money to have their pets buried? How do you know about this place?"

"I . . . work here after school," Eddie answered. He turned suddenly on the man. "Listen, you have to promise us . . ." Eddie said. "If we give you the money, you have to promise us—"

The man erupted. "I don't have to promise you anything, dude!" He gave Eddie a hard shove in the chest with both hands. "Get it?"

Startled, Eddie uttered a cry and stumbled back, into a tree. It took him a few seconds to catch his breath. "Okay. Okay," he muttered.

"Take me to the money," the man growled. "Where did you bury it?"

Eddie motioned with his head. "In a grave over there."

"Dig it up. Hurry," the man said. He turned to me. "Let's get this over with."

What did that mean? Did that mean he planned to kill us?

I struggled to breathe. I had a sudden impulse to scream, to cry for help. But I didn't see anyone around. The grave-yard was empty.

We walked in silence, our shoes scraping the dirt.

"Whoa." Suddenly, Eddie stopped.

The man wheeled around, his body tensing. "What's your problem?"

"I . . . have a shovel in Emmy's trunk," Eddie told him. "I'll need it to dig up the briefcase."

Eddie turned and started back toward the parking lot.

"No way!" the man shouted. "Do you think I'm stupid? You go back to the car and drive off to get help?"

"No," Eddie raised his right hand as if taking a vow. "No. I have to get the shovel."

"Okay. We'll all go get the shovel," the man said. He stepped up beside Eddie and walked with his big hand pressing down on Eddie's shoulder.

I followed close behind, my mind whirring. I knew there was no shovel in my trunk. What was Eddie planning? Did he have some crazy idea?

A crazy idea that was going to get us both shot?

Our shoes crunched over the gravel parking lot. A shadow rolled over us as the lowering afternoon sun van-ished behind trees.

Walking in silence, we approached the car. I uttered a startled gasp as Eddie dove past the trunk. He hurtled to the passenger door and heaved it open.

Before the big man could move, Eddie bent into the car and dropped open the glove compartment.

"Hey, wait—!" the man protested.

Eddie stood up and turned. He raised his arm and I saw the gun wrapped tightly in his fist.

The man shouted a curse and took a step back.

Eddie pointed the gun at the man's broad chest. His hand was shaking, but his voice came out steady, almost calm. "I know how to use this," Eddie said.

The man took another step back, unable to hide his surprise. He stood stiffly, both arms tensed at his sides.

Silence for a long moment. No one moved. Even the wind appeared to stop blowing, and the whisper of the trees hushed.

The man slowly pulled off his sunglasses and tucked them in his jacket pocket. His eyes were narrowed on the gun quavering in Eddie's hand.

"What is that?" he asked Eddie, his voice just above a whisper. "A .38 snubnose?"

Eddie nodded.

The man stared at it for another long moment. Then he said, "Eddie, is that the gun you used when you held up the armored truck?"

34.

My mind spun with confusion. Why was the robber accusing Eddie?

Eddie tightened his grip on the revolver, keeping it aimed at the man's chest. "Is that . . . supposed to be a joke? I didn't rob any truck. You—"

"The security camera clearly showed a snubnose .38," the man said.

Eddie's mouth dropped open. "Security camera? I don't get it."

I suddenly felt dizzy, as if the ground was tilting up to me. I struggled to make sense of this. Any sense at all.

"Eddie, I'm not carrying a gun," the man said. "I'm going to reach very slowly into my back pocket and pull out something I want to show you. Is that okay with you?" He was speaking slowly and carefully.

Eddie nodded. "Okay."

The man did just what he had said. He reached his right hand back slowly and pulled something from his back pocket. At first, I thought it was a wallet. But then he flipped it open.

It had a silvery metal star on one side. Some kind of license beneath it.

"My name is Fairfax," he said, holding the badge holder up so we could both see. "I'm with the Treasury Department. I'm the federal agent assigned to the armored truck robbery."

Eddie and I stared at him. It took a long while for it to sink in. He wasn't the holdup guy. He was a cop.

"We thought—" I started to talk, then stopped myself.

Fairfax's dark eyes slid from me to Eddie. "Sorry I pulled the tough-guy act," he said. "But I had a hunch if I came on strong and scared you enough, I could get something out of you."

"Well, you scared us plenty," I murmured.

Fairfax held out his hand. "Give me the gun, Eddie."

Eddie hesitated for a moment, the gun still pointed at the agent's chest. Then he lowered his arm and handed the revolver to Fairfax.

Fairfax rolled it in his hand, studying it. "Do you want to tell me about the gun, son? I wasn't lying about the security footage we have. A gun just like this was used to hold up the armored truck."

"Well . . . I didn't rob any truck," Eddie said. "I'm seventeen. Do you really think I leave school in the afternoon and go rob armored trucks?"

"We've seen younger," Fairfax muttered. He turned to

me. "Did you know you were carrying a concealed weapon in your car?"

"N-no," I stammered. "No way."

"I can explain it," Eddie said, his eyes on me. "We had an overnight in the woods. The night we discovered the briefcase hidden in the tree. I brought the gun that night. I—"

"Why?" Fairfax interrupted.

"Just to show off, I guess. I shot a raccoon with it. It was stupid. I know."

"And then you stashed the gun in Emmy's glove compartment?" Fairfax asked.

"I put it in there and forgot about it," Eddie replied. "There was so much going on. It was crazy. A crazy night. I . . . I meant to return it. But I totally forgot it was in there. Until just now."

Fairfax's eyes flashed. "Return it to who?"

Eddie hesitated. Of course he didn't want to tell the agent it was Lou's gun.

"Return it to who?" Fairfax repeated the question. He took a menacing step toward Eddie.

Eddie sighed in surrender. "It's my stepfather's gun. I borrowed it. I didn't tell him. I meant to return it. I—"

"Who's your stepfather?" Fairfax demanded.

"He's going to kill me when he learns I borrowed his gun," Eddie said, shaking his head.

"I'm getting tired of having to repeat every question," Fairfax growled. "Who is your stepfather?"

"His name is Lou Kovacs. He's a cop."

Fairfax's face twisted in surprise. "A cop?"

"With the Shadyside precinct," Eddie said. "Only he's suspended. He got in some trouble, and he's waiting for a hearing."

"I'd better pay him a visit," Fairfax said.

"He'll kill me," Eddie repeated in a trembling voice. "He'll just kill me."

I wrapped a hand around Eddie's arm. I wanted to help calm him, but I also needed someone to lean on. This was too frightening, too horrible.

Fairfax kept the revolver lowered at his side. "We're not done here," he said. "Did you forget? We have one more thing we have to do."

35.

"Take me to the money," Fairfax said, gesturing with the revolver. "That's why we came here—right?"

"Okay. Okay," Eddie said softly.

We both knew we had no choice. We had to do whatever the agent told us. Were we both in major trouble because of the gun in my car? I didn't want to think about it. I just wanted to be home, safe, and away from this frightening, stern-faced man.

Fairfax and I followed Eddie into the cemetery, down a long row of gravestones. Eddie began to search around for a shovel.

But before he found one, we heard a shout. I saw Mac Stanton come running from the office, waving both hands. "Hey! Hey!"

His bald head gleamed under the afternoon sunlight. He was dressed in gray sweats. He ran barefoot across the grass. "Hey! What's up?"

Mac was breathing hard by the time he reached us. "Eddie? What are you doing here? You don't work today."

Eddie hesitated. "I . . . well . . ."

Fairfax stepped in front of Eddie. He raised his badge to Mac's sweaty face. "Federal Agent Fairfax," he said.

Mac's mouth dropped open. His eyes went wide as he stared at the badge. He took a step back. "Wh-what do you want?" he stammered.

Mac looks terrified, I realized. Why is he so scared?

"Are you the owner of this place?" Fairfax asked.

Mac nodded. "Yes. If I've done something wrong, I think—"

Fairfax shook his head. "I'm in the middle of an investigation here. If you'd just stand over there." He pointed to a row of graves across the dirt path.

"But if there's a problem—" Mac started.

Fairfax narrowed his eyes at him. "Just step back, sir. Stand over there. We can talk about it in a few minutes."

Mac saw that he had no choice. He squinted at Eddie, as if Eddie might give him a hint as to what was going down.

But Eddie had already found a shovel resting on a tall gravestone. He carried it to the edge of the grave and began to dig, tossing heaps of dirt to the side.

"Am I in trouble? Do I need a lawyer?" Mac called.

Fairfax eyed him suspiciously. "Do you?"

Mac didn't reply. He wiped sweat off his forehead. "You come on my property without a warrant and—"

"Sir, I don't believe this concerns you." Fairfax spoke

slowly, pronouncing each word. I could see he was trying to stay polite, but Mac was annoying him.

"Is this boy in trouble?" Mac demanded. "I can vouch for him."

Fairfax narrowed his eyes at Mac. "Not now."

Eddie groaned with each heave of the shovel. A tall pile of dirt stood at the side of the grave. I saw the brown leather briefcase handle before Eddie did. "There," I said, pointing.

With another groan, Eddie tossed the shovel aside. He jumped into the grave, bent down, and tugged the briefcase up from the dirt.

"What is that? What is that doing there?" Mac cried. "Somebody better tell me what's going on here."

Fairfax ignored him. He moved quickly to take the briefcase from Eddie. Then he motioned for Eddie to step back.

Eddie moved beside me, wiping dirt off his hands on the legs of his jeans. "Are you okay?" I whispered.

He nodded, eyes on the briefcase.

"The money is in here?" Fairfax asked Eddie.

Eddie nodded again. "This is the briefcase Emmy and I found inside a hollow tree in the Fear Street Woods."

Fairfax raised the case. "Well . . . let's take a look. I know a lot of people who will be very glad to know that the money has been retrieved."

"What money? What are we talking about here?" Mac demanded.

Fairfax motioned him back with one hand.

223

He turned the briefcase and, gripping it in one hand, he struggled with the latch. It took a few tries but it finally popped open.

Fairfax tossed back the leather flap. He reached a hand into the briefcase, fumbled around inside, and pulled his hand out quickly.

We all stared at the stack of paper in his fist.

Fairfax peered into the case. Then he raised his eyes to Eddie and me. "No money," he said. "Just stacks of cut-up newspaper."

36.

I uttered a startled gasp. I gripped Eddie's arm as my legs felt about to collapse. Eddie stood staring at the stack of cut-up newspaper in Fairfax's hand, his mouth hanging open in shock.

Mac was the first to speak "I need an explanation here," he said, running over to us. Beads of sweat covered his shaved head. His eyes appeared to roll around crazily revealing his anger and confusion. "You come on my property without a search warrant. You dig up one of my clients' graves. What is going on here, Fairfax? Do I need to lawyer up?"

Fairfax raised a hand, as if to hold Mac back. "Please don't interfere, sir," he said quietly. "This is a federal investigation of an armored truck robbery. Do you know anything that might help me with that?"

Fairfax's words caught Mac by surprise. "M-me?" he sputtered. "Robbery? I don't know anything about that. What does it have to do with me?"

Fairfax raised the briefcase. "Have you ever seen this before?"

Mac shook his head violently. "No. No way. Why was it in a pet grave?"

"I can explain," Eddie broke in. "I put it there, Mac. I—"

Mac's eyes went wide. "You're not involved in a robbery, are you, Eddie? I know you. You would never—"

"He'll explain later, sir," Fairfax said. He clamped the briefcase shut. "Eddie, you're going to have to tell me where this briefcase has been. We're going to have to have a long talk. Someone very carefully replaced the money with newspaper."

Eddie shook his head but didn't reply.

I knew how he felt. This was happening too fast, and it was too confusing. What could we say?

"If Eddie needs money for legal help, contact me," Mac chimed in. "He's a stand-up kid."

"A stand-up kid with a .38 snubnose revolver," Fairfax replied. He motioned us to follow him to my car. "First, we need to talk to the owner of this gun. Take me to your stepfather."

Fairfax drove my car. Eddie gave him the directions to his house. I sat in the backseat, my whole body tensed, my teeth clenched so hard my jaw ached.

Lou didn't do it, I kept repeating to myself. Lou didn't rob the truck. It couldn't have been Lou.

I stared straight ahead at Eddie in the front seat. I tried

to read his thoughts, but his face was a total blank, as if he had shut off, as if he was in some kind of shock.

Eddie pushed open the front door and led us into his house. His Mom and Dad were in the den, a basketball game on the flat-screen TV. They jumped to their feet as we entered.

Lou squinted at us. "Eddie? Emmy? What's up?"

Fairfax held the gun in one hand, the briefcase in the other.

Lou's eyes locked on the briefcase, and his mouth dropped open. "Where'd you find that?" he blurted out.

Fairfax raised the briefcase higher. "Do you recognize it?"

Lou swallowed hard. I could see that he realized he'd made a mistake.

"I'm Federal Agent Fairfax," the agent said. "Are you saying that you recognize this case?"

Lou's whole body slumped, like a balloon deflating. A whoosh of air escaped his open mouth.

"I . . . should have known," he murmured. "How did you find me so fast?"

Fairfax didn't move. "This is your gun and your briefcase?"

Lou nodded. "I should have known. I should have known," he repeated, eyes on the floor. "But I was desperate, you see."

Eddie finally realized what was happening. He uttered a cry.

Fairfax stepped in front of him. "Don't say another word," Fairfax told Lou. "I'm placing you under arrest. You will be read your rights."

Eddie's mom started to sob. She grabbed her husband with both hands and shook him. "Lou, you didn't. You didn't. Tell me you didn't."

Lou covered his face with both hands. "I should have known."

Two days later, Eddie, Sophie, and I sat in my living room. I'd put a big bowl of tortilla chips on the coffee table. But none of us felt like eating. We kept reliving the past few days. Kept discussing it, as if we could talk it away.

"This is so messed up," Eddie said. "I knew Lou was desperate. But I don't think Mom and I had any idea how desperate he really was." Eddie sat beside me on the couch, one arm draped lightly around my shoulders.

Sophie sat on the floor, her legs crossed, her back against the cushion of an armchair. "But . . . robbing an armored truck? Whatever gave him the idea?" she said.

Eddie frowned. "Lou had worked security duty for the company. He knew their schedule. He knew when they'd be making the biggest collection of the week."

He slapped the side of his head. "Who would believe that I'd take the gun he used in a crime? How horrible is that? I . . . feel so bad. I was so stupid. I just wanted to show off. I had no way of knowing . . ." His voice trailed off.

We sat in silence for a while. Sophie leaned forward and

grabbed a handful of chips. Eddie snuggled against me. He squeezed my hand. His hand was ice cold.

"I just can't believe this is happening to my family," he said, his voice breaking. He let go of my hand and lowered his gaze to the floor.

"I can't either," I murmured. I felt so bad for Eddie, but I didn't know what to say. I knew there wasn't anything I could say that might cheer him up.

"I can't believe Lou did it," Eddie said, sighing again. "Remember when you had dinner at my house and Lou showed us that security tape of the truck holdup? It was him on the screen, and he was showing it to us. Why?"

"He must have been testing us," I said. "He wanted to see if we recognized him."

"And we didn't," Eddie said. "We sat there and stared at it, and we didn't have a clue."

Sophie climbed to her feet. She grabbed another handful of chips from the bowl. "So where is the money?" she asked.

Eddie and I stared at her. "We . . . don't know," I said.

"The police said Lou's charges could be reduced if he returned the money," Sophie said.

"Lou swears he doesn't have it and he doesn't know where it is," Eddie said.

"Do the police believe him?" Sophie asked.

"How should I know?" Eddie snapped. He squeezed my hand so hard, it hurt. I tugged myself free. "How should I know what the police believe?" he shouted. "They believe my stepfather is a criminal. That's what the cops believe. And he is. Lou is going to prison whether he has the money or not. And what will become of Mom and me? That's the real question, Sophie."

He was breathing hard from his outburst, his face red. I reached to comfort him, but he pulled away.

"Sorry," Sophie said, rolling her eyes. "I asked the wrong question. Sorry. You don't have to bite my head off."

Eddie glared at her.

"I think I know where the money is," I said.

They both turned to me. Sophie dropped her tortilla chips back into the bowl. Her eyes were wide with surprise.

"Where?" Eddie said.

"I think Mac has the money," I said. "He—"

"Huh? Are you kidding me?" Eddie said. "Mac doesn't know anything about anything. He doesn't—"

I grabbed his wrist. "Shut up and listen to me. The night we buried the briefcase for the first time? I had a feeling someone was watching us. And I remember the lights were on in Mac's office."

Eddie narrowed his eyes at me. "So?"

"I think Mac watched us bury the briefcase. The first time. And maybe he was watching the second time we buried it. And after we left, he dug it up, took the money, and replaced it with newspaper strips."

Eddie shook his head. "But you saw Mac's reaction when that federal agent made us dig up the case. Mac didn't have a clue. He didn't know what was going on."

"He could have been faking that," I said. "It's easy to play innocent, Eddie."

"Sure, it is. I do it all the time!" Sophie chimed in.

It was a joke, but Eddie and I just ignored her. I could see Eddie was thinking hard.

"Think about when we dug up the briefcase," I said. "Remember how strange Mac acted? He looked frightened. Really. And he kept asking Fairfax if he needed to get a lawyer."

"I remember," Eddie said thoughtfully. "Yes. He did act frightened."

"Like he thought the agent was there to investigate him," I continued. "Why? Why was Mac so weird? Maybe because he had something to hide."

"Like the money," Eddie said. "The money from the briefcase."

Eddie thought about it some more. "I sure would love to help Lou. If we found that money and returned it. . . ."

"When can we search Mac's office?" I said. "And his apartment upstairs?"

Eddie scratched his head. "What day is it? Friday? That's good. Mac always goes to stay with his girlfriend on Friday. We can go now."

"Can I come, too?" Sophie asked. "I can help search. Or I could be lookout. Three heads are better than two."

"Not a good idea," I replied. "It could be dangerous, Sophie, and—"

I saw the hurt expression on her face. Here I was, shutting

her out again. Not letting her help. Not letting her be part of the danger.

"Okay, okay," I said.

So, the three of us drove to the pet cemetery, broke into Mac's office, and started to search for the money.

And yes, we found the danger we thought we might encounter there. But it was much more horrifying than any of us could have predicted.

37.

Mac kept his office simple and neat. His desk had a stack of folders on one corner and a framed photo of a German shepherd on the other. A white coffee mug held a bunch of ballpoint pens.

A table beside the desk held a laptop computer, open to its home screen, only a few icons visible. An old-fashioned black telephone sat beside the laptop. Next to it, a glass jar of hard peppermints.

A wooden visitors' chair across from the desk, a bookshelf, and a single file cabinet against the back were the only other furniture. The walls were covered with framed snapshots of dogs and cats.

Eddie and I pawed through the desk drawers. They were as neat and uncluttered as the rest of the office. Sophie dropped to her knees and began to search the bottom filing cabinet drawers.

"Maybe he has a hidden wall safe," I said, gazing around the office.

"How could it be hidden?" Eddie said. "There's nothing to hide it behind."

The walls were plasterboard painted white. I walked all the way around, smoothing my hands over the wall, searching behind some of the framed snapshots. No hidden compartments. Nowhere a safe could be hidden.

"These drawers just have old contracts and bills and stuff," Sophie reported. She climbed to her feet and pulled open the top drawer. "A thermos and a first-aid kit and a bunch of wires and cables," she reported. "And look." She held up a big jar of marshmallow fluff. "How weird is this?"

"Lots of people are into marshmallow fluff," I said.

"Nothing here. Let's try the backroom," Eddie said.

Sophie and I followed him through the narrow doorway. He clicked on a ceiling light. Of course, I'd been here before with Eddie. It was a small, cramped storage room with stacks of cardboard cartons, some old office furniture, folding chairs, two broken shovels leaning against an old couch.

I gazed at the glare from the video screens against one wall. They sat on a table with the other security camera equipment. On the screens, I could see dark graves and trees outside. Nothing moved.

"What are those cups for?" Sophie pointed to shelves of metal cups, dozens of them lined up neatly in rows. "Are they sports trophies?"

"Those aren't trophy cups," Eddie said. "They're urns.

You know. That's where the ashes go when Mac cremates a dog or cat."

Sophie made a disgusted face. "You mean people walk in with a dog or a cat and they walk out with a silver cup full of ashes?"

Eddie nodded. "What did you think went on here, Sophie? Did you think it was like a day spa or a grooming salon?"

"Stop snapping at me," Sophie said. "I came here to help you, remember? It's not my fault that you work in a totally creepy place."

"Let's just search and get out of here," I said. The tension between Sophie and Eddie was starting to get to me. I knew it wasn't really Sophie's fault. And Eddie had good reason to be tense and angry.

We squeezed between the stacks of cartons, but didn't find any place where money could be hidden. Eddie pulled open a few cartons at the top of the stacks. One of them contained bags of gravel. Another held bottles of chemicals.

"We need to go upstairs and search Mac's apartment," he said.

He clicked off the ceiling light. I gasped as I heard a hard bump. From the front office. I couldn't see Eddie and Sophie in the darkness. But I froze. My breath caught in my throat.

Was someone at the front door? Was Mac back?

I heard Eddie move. My eyes slowly adjusted to the

dark. I followed him to the doorway of the backroom and, still holding my breath, gazed toward the front.

The office door was glass. I squinted out into the night.

Another bump at the door. And I saw the black Lab butting his snout against the glass. His eyes glowed darkly as he peered in at us. He pawed the dirt in front of the door and banged the glass once again with his head.

"Good watchdog," Sophie muttered.

I let out a tense laugh. "How many times is that dog going to scare me?"

Once again, I thought of the black wolf from my dreams. No matter where I was or how tense or how involved in something else, my dreams were always nearby, always nagging at the back of my mind. Along with Aunt Marta's terrifying words: "You are wolfen."

"Ignore the dog. He can't get in," Eddie said, putting his hands on my waist and turning me toward the metal stairway at the side of the front office. "Let's go upstairs and get this over with."

I stood frozen for another moment. I still wasn't breathing normally from the scare that dog gave me. To my surprise, Eddie leaned forward and kissed my cheek. "You'll be okay," he whispered.

The touch of his lips made my skin tingle. I saw Sophie watching from the back-room doorway.

Our shoes made clanging noises as we climbed the metal rungs to Mac's living quarters. We stepped into a small bedroom filled up mostly with a king-sized bed. The blanket and sheets were tossed in a pile at the foot of the bed. Shirts and jeans cluttered the floor and were draped over a wooden chair. A small flat-screen TV stood on a long, low dresser at the foot of the bed.

Eddie clicked on the bedside table lamp, and we quickly went through the dresser drawers, searched the small clothes closet, and explored the space under the bed.

No luck.

We were down to our last room to search, a small front room with a couch piled with books and magazines, a low table cluttered with empty beer bottles.

"If the money isn't here . . ." Sophie started.

"It doesn't mean that Mac didn't take it," I insisted. "Maybe he hid the money somewhere else. Maybe he buried it in a grave like we did."

"Or maybe he didn't take it," Eddie said. "Maybe we got it all wrong."

"Maybe," I admitted.

I moved to the back of the desk and, crouching, slid out the bottom drawer. It was empty. I stared at it. The drawer was shallow, not very long at all.

"Something weird here," I muttered. I pulled the drawer all the way out and set it down on the floor. Then I lowered my head and peered into the opening. "Hey—!"

I spotted another drawer behind the shallow one. A hidden drawer?

I leaned forward, reached all the way in, grabbed the handle, and tugged. This drawer was a lot heavier than I imagined. It didn't slide out easily. I tugged again.

Eddie and Sophie had turned to watch me. The hidden drawer was long. I pulled it halfway out and gazed down at it. Gazed down at the stacks of hundred-dollar bills. Neat piles of bills, wrapped in small bunches with rubber bands.

"Oh, wow."

Eddie and Sophie were leaning over me now. "You found it," Eddie said.

"Maybe it's Mac's money," Sophie said. "Maybe it isn't the stolen money."

"Then why would he hide it in a secret drawer?" I asked. "Who keeps stacks of one hundreds in their house?" I picked up a thick stack and flipped my fingers through it. "This is it. I knew it. I knew Mac saw us. He must have dug up the briefcase as soon as we left, and he took the money."

Eddie let out a long breath. His eyes were on the drawer. "This is excellent. This is really going to help Lou."

I stood up and pulled out my phone. "I'll call the police. I'll tell them we found the stolen money. I guess we have to wait for them to come . . ."

I crossed to the doorway where the light was better. I raised the phone and squinted at the screen.

"Owww!" I cried out as a hard slap sent the phone flying from my hand. It bounced against the wall and dropped to the floor. I pulled back my hand—and stared at Mac.

His face was dark with anger, his eyes wide, teeth clenched. He shoved me aside and stomped into the room. "So sorry," he said softly. "So sorry it has to be this way."

38.

Mac's words sent a chill to the back of my neck. "You—you can't keep us here!" I cried. I dove to the doorway, but he moved quickly, blocked my path, and I bounced off him.

I stumbled back. "L-let us out of here!" I stammered.

Mac clicked the door lock. "Let's be calm and think about this," he said. He stepped to the desk, pulled open the middle drawer, and his hand came out gripping a small pistol. "Maybe this will help you three stay calm." He aimed it at Eddie, then, Sophie, then me.

"Mac, we know you took the money," Eddie said. "The police—"

"Shut up!" Mac screamed. He lowered the gun till it was pointed at Eddie's chest. "Just shut up." He nodded his shaved head a few times. Beads of sweat had formed on his forehead. "Okay. Okay. We have a problem here." He was talking to himself.

His eyes darted rapidly from side to side. I could see

that he was thinking hard, desperate to come up with a plan.

"You're not going to shoot us," I said.

He waved the pistol. "Shut up. I mean it. Just shut up." He turned his gaze on Eddie. "I like you, kid. You know that. You're my cousin's son. You're family. But I can't let you ruin everything for me. The money is mine now, and I plan to keep it." He rubbed his shaved head with his free hand. "But what am I going to do with the three of you?"

We stood there in that small room, the money at our feet. No one moved. Our eyes were all on Mac. My legs were trembling, and it felt as if my heart had jumped into my throat. I struggled to breathe.

He wouldn't kill us, would he? He wouldn't kill us for the money."

"Follow me," he said, waving the gun again. "Follow me and don't say a word." He gave Eddie's shoulder a hard shove. "Don't try anything."

"Mac, listen," Eddie pleaded. "You don't want to hurt my stepfather, do you? Lou is going to do a lot of prison time if that money isn't returned."

Mac shoved Eddie again, sending him stumbling into the wall. "Lou made his bed. Now he has to sleep in it. It doesn't mean I have to be a loser, too."

He forced us out the door and down the metal stairway. "Keep moving," he barked. "Out the back door. This way. Hurry."

"Where are you taking us?" Sophie demanded.

"Shut up," Mac said again. "I have to think. I need time to think."

He forced us out a narrow door at the back of the supply room. We were outside now, but in a walled-in area I'd never seen before. I waited for my eyes to adjust to the light and then gazed around.

"Ohhh, the smell," Sophie groaned. She pinched her fingers over her nose.

The sour putrid odor filled my nose. Much stronger back here. So strong, it made my eyes water. I grabbed my stomach as it started to lurch.

What smells so bad back here?

"Get moving," Mac ordered. "Walk!"

Tall brick walls on both sides of us. Huddled close together, we made our way through the narrow gravel path between the walls. I could see the pale half-moon above us in the night sky, but I couldn't see anything else over the high walls.

"I'm going to be sick," Sophie moaned. "I . . . I can't stand the smell. Ohhhhh noooo." She bent over as if about to puke.

Mac gave her a shove that sent her sprawling to her knees. "Walk. Walk and shut up. You'll have plenty of time to discuss the smell in a moment."

"This is seriously crazy, Mac," Eddie said. "Where are you taking us? Why don't you just take the money, get in your Jeep, and take off?"

"Maybe I will," Mac said. "You're smart, Eddie. Maybe

that's just what I'll do. Take the money and get as far away from here as I can."

The gravel path wasn't very long. We stopped at the end. The odor was so powerful here, I couldn't breathe at all. The smell was sickening, like nothing I'd ever smelled before. I wiped tears from my eyes and struggled to hold my breath. Every muscle in my body tensed tightly.

"That's just what I'm going to do," Mac said. "I'm outta here. But I need a little time to get it together. So I need to put you away for a while."

Put us away? What did that mean?

"Go ahead. Jump," Mac said, his jaw clenched, his face beaded with large drops of sweat. "Jump. All of you."

I suddenly realized that the three of us were standing at the edge of a pit. A deep hole in the ground. I peered over the edge, but I couldn't see the bottom.

"How deep is it? What's down there?" Sophie demanded in a trembling voice, her eyes wide with fear.

"Go find out," Mac said. He shoved her from behind and sent her toppling into the pit. I gripped the sides of my face and screamed in horror as she vanished.

Sophie's scream joined mine. We heard a soft *splat* as she landed.

"No . . . no . . . no . . ." I kept repeating, shaking my head, my hands still pressed to my cheeks.

"Go ahead. Join her," Mac screamed. "Jump! Jump in!"

Eddie and I hesitated at the edge. My legs were shaking

so hard, I could barely stand. I cupped my hands around my mouth and called down: "Sophie? Are you okay?"

No answer.

"Mac, give us a break," Eddie said. Moving suddenly, he lowered his shoulder and rammed it deep into Mac's big belly.

Mac uttered a groan. The pistol flew from his hand. Gasping for breath, Mac dove for it. Eddie dropped to his knees. Reached for the pistol. And Mac kicked him hard in the side.

"Stop! Stop!" I shrieked. I stumbled back from the pit edge, my eyes on the gun.

With a sharp cry, Eddie tried to roll away from Mac. But Mac kicked him again, with even more force, a fierce kick that made Eddie scream in pain.

The force of the kick sent Eddie rolling over the side and into the pit. Another soft *splat* sound made me gasp.

Mac grabbed the pistol, spun around, his eyes wild, his chest heaving up and down. "You made me do that!" he shouted. "I didn't want to fight you, Eddie." He aimed the gun at me.

I shut my eyes—stepped over the edge, and dropped into the pit.

39.

I landed on my back with a sharp cry. My breath whooshed out and my lungs throbbed with sharp pain. Fighting the pain, I struggled to regain my breathing. I glanced around. I saw Sophie and Eddie climb to their knees.

"Emmy—Emmy—are you okay?" Eddie cried, reaching toward me with both hands.

"I-I think so," I stammered.

I swung myself onto my stomach and started to pull myself up. I stopped when I realized my hands were buried in something soft. Some kind of fur?

I raised my hands and bumped something hard. A tree branch? No. I raised it close and saw that it was a bone, a bone with patches of fur clinging to it.

An animal bone. I waved it in the air. "Eddie—look!"

"A dog's leg!" he cried.

"Oh, nooo!" A cry burst from my throat, and I heaved it to the pit bottom.

Trembling in horror, I gazed down at the bones poking

up from the clumps of fur beneath me. "I . . . I think these are ribs!" I choked out.

Her eyes wide with terror, Sophie raised a skull in one hand. "It's . . . it's . . . a dog skull."

"Oh, no. Oh, no. Oh, no." The moans escaped my throat as I realized we were sitting on top of corpses. Dead dogs and cats. It all started to come into focus. Patches of ragged fur. Rib bones and leg bones and skulls with their eye sockets black and empty.

"Oh, no. Oh, no." I shifted my weight. My hand tightened around something beneath me, and I raised it to my face. A dog tail. A long fur-covered dog tail.

"Noooooo!" A scream burst from deep inside me. I heaved the tail against the pit wall. I tried to stand, tried to move to Sophie and Eddie. Stumbled. Fell back into the deep pile of corpses. Rotting meat . . . tattered fur . . . clumps of bones. Flies buzzing, swarming so thick and dark they blocked out the moonlight.

"The smell," Eddie uttered in a hoarse whisper. "Now we know. Now we know where the smell comes from."

"But . . . what is this pit?" I screamed in a trembling voice.

"Don't you see?" Sophie cried. "Mac never buried the animals. He never cremated them or anything."

She staggered over the bodies to the dirt pit wall and pressed her back against it. "He never cremated them and he never buried them. He took people's money, and he just tossed the dead pets into this pit."

I pulled a chunk of hardened meat from the back of my

T-shirt. My hair felt wet. I didn't want to think about what caused it. Wave after wave of nausea rolled down my body. I brushed chunks of fur-covered flesh off the legs of my jeans.

Sophie tugged something from her hair. "What is this?" she shrieked. "Ohmigod! Ohmigod! It's a heart or a liver or something!" She tossed it to the pit floor.

Eddie stumbled to the dirt wall. He tried to grip the side and pull himself up. But the soft dirt tumbled from under his hands and he slid back down. He made his way to Sophie. "This explains why Mac was so frightened when that federal agent came to the cemetery. Mac thought this pit had been discovered. He thought he'd been caught cheating his customers."

Flies swarmed around my head. I tried to bat them away with both hands. "No. That's not it," I said. "Mac was afraid the agent knew Mac had taken the stolen money."

"Hey—!" Mac leaned over the edge of the pit and scowled down at us. "Did I hear someone saying my name in vain?"

"Let us out! Let us out of here!" I screamed. Sophie and Eddie repeated my plea.

"No way," Mac shouted down to us. "You can stay down there till I get away."

"Get away?" I cried.

He stuck his face over the pit edge. He was drenched in sweat, and he kept blinking crazily, as if he'd lost control of his eyelids. Tension, I guessed.

"I'm taking your advice. I'm grabbing the money and getting out of here. I'll be rich somewhere else," he said. "Somewhere far away from here."

"But you can't leave us down here!" Eddie cried.

"Don't worry about it," Mac replied. "Someone will find you. In a day or two probably." That made him chuckle. Awesome joke.

We shouted and pleaded. But he disappeared.

Eddie covered his head in his hands. I swung my arms rapidly, still trying to bat away the swarming flies. Sophie leaned against the pit wall, her mouth hanging open, not moving, still as a statue.

Over the buzzing drone of the flies, I listened to the silence above the pit. Mac had definitely gone. He wasn't up there listening to us. He wasn't going to rescue us from this putrid horror.

Angrily, I kicked a slender cat skull with my shoe. It made a clattering sound as it landed inside upturned rib bones, some of the meat and fur still clinging.

My eyes studied the dirt wall. Too steep and too high to climb. Eddie had already tried, but he couldn't climb the side. But maybe if one of us gave a boost to another . . . maybe if we did some kind of pyramid thing . . . maybe we could push one of us out, and they could rescue the remaining two. . . .

My mind was spinning. There had to be a way for at least one of us to get to the top.

"Eddie?" I started to ask him if he had any ideas on how we could escape.

But then Sophie caught my eye. Something strange. Something strange was happening to my sister.

Gripped in shock, I stared silently as her face began to change. Her eyes grew bigger, darker. Her nose pressed into her skin, and a long snout poked through. A long animal snout.

I wanted to call out to her. But I couldn't find my voice. I couldn't find words.

And I watched, paralyzed, as the black fur spread over Sophie's arms, her legs . . . in seconds she was covered in thick animal fur. Pointed ears poked from the top of her fur-covered head. She pulled back black lips revealing two sets of yellow teeth . . . curled fangs poking down to her chin. She snapped her jaw . . . snapped her teeth, as if testing them. Dropped to her knees. Raised herself on four clawed animal paws, pawing the dirt, snapping her jaw.

"Sophie—" I uttered her name. I finally found my voice and choked out her name. "Sophie—"

"Emmy . . ." She growled my name, in a husky voice from deep in her throat. "Emmy . . . I'm the wolf! Not you!"

40.

N-no—!" I staggered back, away from her. I lost my balance, stumbled and toppled down, onto a soft, squishy pile of animal fur and bones. I didn't move. I sat there staring at the wolf with its chest heaving, saliva rolling off its fangs.

"Listen to me," Sophie growled a husky, throaty rasp. "I can't talk long. Listen to me before the transformation is complete."

I stared at her—stared at this terrifying wolf creature that was my sister—stared at her, unable to speak.

"When you had those wolf dreams," Sophie snarled, "you thought you were dreaming about yourself. But now you see the truth. You were dreaming about ME!"

"I-I don't understand," I stammered. Across from me, Eddie had his back pressed to the dirt pit wall, his mouth hanging open in shock. "Sophie, why—"

Sophie didn't give me a chance to finish my question.

With a fierce growl, she arched her spine, pulled back on her hind legs, bared her fangs—and leaped at me.

I screamed in horror. I raised my hands as a shield and ducked my head.

But Sophie wasn't attacking me. She leaped over me. Her forepaws grabbed the top of the pit easily, and her belly rubbed the side as she hoisted herself out of the hole, kicking hard with her hind legs.

Eddie and I didn't move. It was as if we were frozen in horror, in shock.

Sophie . . . my sister . . .

I heard the heavy *thud* of her paws on the ground above us.

Then I heard Mac's scream. The scream cut off sharply. I heard a struggle. Grunts. Groans.

Eddie and I both cried out as Mac came hurtling down into the pit. He landed between us on his back. He bounced once, sending animal parts and patches of fur flying. His t-shirt was torn to shreds and blood puddled down his chest.

"Help me . . . Hellllp me," he groaned, gazing up at me, eyes bulging in terror.

Before he could struggle to his feet, the wolf came leaping in after him. She landed on top of him, shoving him down deep into the corpses with her front paws. He raised both hands in a futile attempt to shove her away.

But Sophie lowered her teeth to his chest, tore away a large piece of skin, shook it in her teeth, and tossed it aside.

Then she raised her snout to Mac's throat—and bit deeply, sending up a spray of dark blood that spattered Eddie and me.

Mac stopped struggling. His body went limp, sprawled on his back, covered with bones and fur and dried animal parts.

Panting, Sophie backed off. She kept her head low, waiting to catch her breath. Her dark fur was stained by patches of Mac's blood. Her tongue swept over her fangs, and I knew she tasted his blood on them.

Eddie pressed his back against the pit wall. His eyes, wide with horror, kept darting from Sophie to me. He appeared too frightened to speak.

Finally, I found the courage to talk to her. "Sophie . . . I don't understand any of this. Can you tell me—"

She raised her head. Her blue wolf eyes gleamed as she gazed at me. She began to change again. I could see her face emerge. Sophie's face. Her cheeks . . . her lips. But she remained on all fours, her body covered in thick wolf fur. Sophie's face on a wolf body. Sophie . . . Sophie . . .

"I thought I was the one," I choked out. "I thought I was the wolfen one."

"Marta never could tell us apart," Sophie said in that hoarse growl from deep inside her. "She was half-blind, remember?"

I swallowed. Hugged myself to stop my shudders. "So when we visited Marta when we were l-little . . ." I stammered. "You were the one bitten by a wolf? Not me?"

255

She nodded, still breathing noisily. "Marta told Mom you were bitten. Mom never knew the truth. But I did." She uttered a low growl. "I felt strange my whole life, Emmy. But my wolfen powers didn't bloom until a few months ago."

I shut my eyes, trying to understand all this, struggling to have it make sense. "But all those dreams I had, Sophie. . . . I had the wolf dreams—not you."

"The wolfen powers are strange," Sophie replied. "It took me a while to explore them. It took me a while to figure out how to send you those dreams. It took me a while to figure out how to make you black out . . . how to make you think you were the wolf."

"But . . . why?" I choked out.

"Because you were normal and I was not. It wasn't fair, Emmy. It was never fair. I was just three years old when I was bitten. You should have protected me. You should have helped me."

"But—I was just a little kid, too," I protested.

Sophie turned away from me. She raised her head to the sky.

"Wait—don't go," I begged. "You haven't explained, Sophie. Why did you kill Riley? Why?"

A growl escaped her throat. Again, she turned her gleaming blue eyes on me. "He knew my secret. He was in the park the night I attacked that dog. He recognized me when I turned back into myself. He said he was going to tell. I begged him. But he refused to keep my secret. I couldn't let him tell people. The wolf in me took over. Riley had to die."

I took a deep breath, fighting to slow my racing heart-beats. "And so you made me think that I was the one who killed him?"

"Why should I be the only one whose life is ruined?" she snarled. "Why should I be running on all fours, kill-ing, craving meat like a low animal, while you're totally normal, out having fun with your boyfriend and your friends?"

She growled again. Her eyes went dim. She seemed to sink in on herself, as if her thoughts were too heavy, too frightening to bear.

I reached both hands out to her. I struggled to step across the animal corpses to reach her, to hug her.

But another low growl made me stop. She lowered her head. To attack me? Was she about to leap at me?

No. I cried out as I saw the tears in her eyes. Sophie's tears ran down her face. I glimpsed the tears just for a mo-ment, and I thought my heart would break.

My sister . . . my poor little sister . . .

And then she whipped her head around. As if she didn't want me to see. As if she didn't want me to see the true emotion, the teardrops sliding down her face.

"Goodbye, Emmy," she uttered. "Goodbye. I have to go now."

"No. Sophie—wait," I pleaded. "Where are you going? Where?"

She didn't answer. She arched her spine again. And her face disappeared. Sophie's face melted back into the face of a wolf. She turned to gaze at me for one more brief moment, her eyes peering at me behind the long wolfen snout. Then she coiled her hind legs—and leaped out of the pit.

"Sophie? Where are you going?" I called. "Sophie? Come back!"

Eddie and I stared across the pit at one another and listened to the thunder of her paws as the wolf ran away.

41.

Eddie and I started to scream for help. But we knew it was of no use. We were too deep in the cemetery for anyone to hear us. After a few minutes, we gave up. We hugged each other, held each other tight. We were both trembling . . . from the fright . . . from the horror . . . and from the shock.

We both cried out in surprise when two confused police officers appeared overhead. They quickly pulled Eddie and me from the pit. They lifted Mac carefully and stretched him out on his back on the ground. Then they called for emergency medical help.

One of the officers was having a hard time with the overpowering odor, and once we were rescued, hurried away to throw up against a tree.

Eddie and I held onto each other, shaken but okay. Sophie's hoarse wolf voice lingered in my ears, and I gazed around the cemetery searching for her. But she was gone.

Gone forever?

The two officers had been called by a neighbor who had been walking her dog by the cemetery wall and had heard our screams. Of course, the officers had a million questions: What were we doing here at night? How did we get down in that pit? And why did the pit exist? How did Mac get so badly injured?

To my surprise, Mac was still alive. His neck and chest were caked with blood. His t-shirt and pants had been clawed to pieces. He raised his head, his eyes dazed. He tried to focus on Eddie and me, but I don't think he saw us clearly.

"That wolf . . ." he murmured in a whisper. "That wolf . . ."

One of the officers, a tall young guy with short blond hair, blue eyes, and a nice tan, gently pushed Mac back down. "Don't try to talk. The EMT will be here in a minute or two."

Mac settled back with a sigh and shut his eyes.

The officer turned to Eddie and me. "Did he say a wolf? Maybe the same wolf that attacked that dog in Shadyside Park?"

I shook my head. "I didn't see a wolf," I lied.

"Me, either," Eddie said, lying, too. "We heard some kind of fight. Above us. But we couldn't see anything from down in the pit. Then Mac came falling down, all bloody and messed up."

The cop squinted at us. "You didn't see a wolf?"

We both shook our heads. "No wolf."

"The guy must be delirious," the cop concluded.

Later, as we walked through the pet cemetery to the patrol car parked outside the gate, I gazed at the wolf tracks in the dirt path. Followed them with my eyes as we walked—and wondered if I would ever see Sophie again?

The police called for our parents, and we spent the rest of the night in the Shadyside precinct station. Of course, Mom and Dad were beyond horrified to learn that Eddie and I were in so much danger. They didn't ask about Sophie. They didn't know that Sophie had been with us.

I tried my best to answer all the questions. But the whole time, I had only one thought in my head: How will I ever tell Mom and Dad the truth about Sophie?

Agent Fairfax from the Feds showed up near morning. The money had been retrieved from Mac's desk drawer. He said that would make things easier for Lou. And Fairfax surprised us by announcing that Eddie and I would receive a five-thousand-dollar reward for the return of the money.

I guess they expected me to be excited about that and shout for joy or something. I mean, it was a nice reward. But, where does five thousand dollars compare to losing your sister?

I could see that Eddie felt as exhausted and numb as I did. By the time we had answered all their questions, all the horror of the night before was just starting to sink in. I wanted to cry and scream and go berserk all at once. I honestly felt like I was going to burst apart.

Outside the precinct station, I hugged Eddie, a long hug, pressing my cheek against his. "Talk to you later," he whispered, and he turned to follow his mom.

"I—I—" I wanted to start to explain about Sophie. But Mom put a hand over my mouth to silence me. "You've been through so much, and you've been up all night. We'll talk about everything later," Mom said, holding the car door for me.

Dad slid behind the wheel. "Eddie's stepfather is going to prison for a long time," he said. "He was foolish to think—"

"Not now, Jason!" Mom cried, slapping his arm. "Stop it. This isn't the right time."

We drove home in silence. The whole while I was thinking, when is the right time to talk about Sophie? When?

I didn't want to cry in front of my parents. I couldn't bear to sit there crying in the car. But the tears formed in my eyes and rolled down my cheeks, and I bit my lips to keep from making a sound.

I dreaded stepping into the house, walking into a house with no sister. But I pulled open the kitchen door and stepped inside—and stared at Sophie standing at the sink, washing off a dark purple plum.

She turned as I walked in. She must have heard me gasp.

"Where've you been?" Sophie asked. "I've been texting you for hours."

"Huh?" I stared at her, stared hard as if she was some kind of mirage. Like I had lost my mind, or I was dreaming again. "Sophie? You're really here?"

Sophie dried off the plum with a paper towel. "I told Mom and Dad I was staying over at Libby Howard's last night. Didn't they tell you?"

"With everything that went on, I forgot," Mom said.

Sophie raised her eyebrows. "What happened? I miss everything," she whined.

What an awesome actress she is! I thought. Our parents think she was having a sleepover. They don't know anything.

"You missed everything," Dad told her. "Emmy nearly got herself killed at the pet cemetery last night, but she's okay now."

"We'll talk about it later," Mom said. "Emmy, go to your room. Take a long nap. I know you need it . . . you've been up all night"

Sophie followed me to our bedroom. She grabbed me and pressed her face close to mine. "I decided I don't want to live in the woods," she whispered, her hot breath brushing my ear. "I want to live at home. I don't want to live outside like an animal."

"That's good," I said. I didn't know what else to say.

She squeezed my shoulders, holding me tightly. "I just

have one important question to ask you," she whispered, her eyes locked on mine.

"Question?" I repeated in a tiny voice.

She nodded. "Can you keep a secret?"